I0603224

BANSHEE CRY

BLOOD FAE CHRONICLES
BOOK 1

USA TODAY BEST SELLING AUTHOR
JEN KATEMI

Contents

Banshee Cry (The Blood Fae Chronicles)
Copyright © 2020 Jen Katemi

All rights reserved

ISBN-13: 978-0-6484045-4-5

First Print Edition
Published by Jen Katemi (Flourish Books)

No part of this book may be reproduced or transmitted in any form or
by any means, electronic or mechanical, including photocopying,
recording, or by any information storage and retrieval system, without
permission in writing from the publisher.
This is a work of fiction. Names, places, characters and incidents are
either the product of the author's imagination or are used fictitiously,
and any resemblance to any actual persons, living or dead,
organizations, events or locales is entirely coincidental.

Chapter One

ALEAH

What the hell use is a banshee without a voice?

Well, I do have a voice, sort of, but it's muted and soft. Useless when it comes to sounding a warning. Deadly in its ineffectiveness when the only thing you can do is wail quietly into your pillow while death swoops in downstairs and takes away your father.

I was told by my aunt it took two vamps that night, to slowly suck the lifeblood from my dad. He put up a fight, once he knew what they were. But I didn't give him the warning he needed and when they knocked, he was expecting our neighbors.

He just called out for them to come on in, while I lay in bed upstairs, feeling death rolling in like a wave of agony. Wailing in a whisper, and not even knowing why until it was over.

Four years old and my first death.

By far, the worst banshee experience I've ever had. And all because of the vamps. All because I had no voice.

Now there's a vamp on my front doorstep, begging for help, and all I want to do is stake him. Right through his cold, undead heart.

I stare into the set of icy blue eyes waiting for my response, and the twenty-five-year-old memories of my dad come rushing back in as if it all happened yesterday. The wail rises in my chest, as if called forth simply by the *thought* of death. *No. Not again. Twice in less than twenty-four hours is simply too much to bear.*

My fingers twitch toward the stake that sits looped in my belt but I manage to control the twin urges to scream and stab, and instead take a small step back from the injured vampire standing at my door.

"No." I shake my head for emphasis. "You may *not* enter my home."

"Please." His gaze flickers and I know he's aware of my weapon. "I was...attacked, and now that the sun is on the rise, I need shelter in order to heal. I need—"

"You're hungry."

"No, I—"

"You need to feed."

"I do *not*." His voice rises briefly in obvious annoyance, and then he staggers slightly as if even that faint expending of energy is too much. "I happened to be in the Hatton Grove area for work, and yours is the nearest dwelling. I—"

Work?

"What sort of work nets you a seriously mangled arm and..." I study the unnatural way he's cradling himself. "Your shoulder too. Is it—"

"Dislocated, yes. And I think, maybe, a broken rib or two. I'm with the police. I was after a rogue supe reported near here, but..." He shakes his head as if he's annoyed with himself. "Turns out there are more than one. In this case it was a vamp and a shifter, working together. They got the better of me. This time."

Despite his injury, the words are fierce and a strange reddish glow appears deep behind his eyes. This guy is *pissed*. For a moment, I see beyond the vamp label, and realize the man standing before me is one of the sexiest I've ever laid eyes on.

He's the quintessential tall, dark, and handsome, with rakish hair, an angular facial structure, and a wide, sensual mouth that calls out to be kissed. I find myself leaning close toward him, and quickly recoil instead, blinking hard to try and dispel the allure.

I clench my teeth together and force myself to look away. What the hell am I doing, conversing with a vamp? Even one who may be on the right side of the law. Why am I entertaining this story that may or may not be true?

Since the Accord thirty or so years ago, I've heard of supernatural beings joining mainstream humans in the workforce, but out here on the farm in my little neck of the woods, it's rare to come across any creature

—human or non-human alike. Which is just the way I like it. I don't have to remember my past unless I conjure it up myself – a penance I force myself to pay even decades later.

I take a deep breath. He's wasting my time, and I want to get away before he can pull me in further. The last thing I need is to be tempted by a creature like him. "Get *off* my porch!"

Reluctantly, he backs away. He has no choice, now that I've compelled him. Vamps can't enter without permission and my porch is technically still under my roof. Though only just, which is why he made it all the way to the kitchen entrance.

"The sun's up," he says. There's a tremor in his voice that proves he's worried. I'm not sure if he expects an instant invitation into my home, but it sounds like he assumed at least some form of sympathy might be forthcoming. "You're sending me to my death."

"I'm not." *I would know if death is imminent.*

At least, I'm supposed to know. I should be able to detect such things, and this vampire is not going to die today in the sunlight.

I don't say that out loud but his gaze sharpens, as if he senses something other than mortal.

"You don't care either way, do you?" he asks, cocking his head to the side. Now that he's further away, he narrows his eyes as though trying to make out where that sense of *other* emanates from.

"Oh, yes." I shift under his penetrating gaze, grinding my teeth to keep from growling at his accusations. Sudden anger burns through me and I'm sure spots of pink decorate my cheeks. "I care. I care a great deal."

His gaze drops briefly to where my fist clenches and unclenches beside my stake. Maybe if I remove it —maybe if he sees the gleam of sunlight on the sharp edge of the weapon—he'll take what I have to say more seriously. He won't continue to push.

He nods once. "So be it. I'll try and find a shed. Or something."

He staggers down the porch steps. At the base, he collapses in a motionless heap.

I watch his limp body, waiting for him to slink off. His whole act isn't going to work. I'd be a fool to fall for something so obvious.

And yet, he doesn't move.

Fuck it. Fuck it to fucking hell and back.

If he stays there, he *will* die, wound or no wound. Do I stand and watch and wail in semi-silence while death creeps in and takes him? Do I venture out there and hasten his passing with my stake? I am tempted.

What if it's just a trick? If he truly is hungry, my blood will call to him far more strongly than any pure-bred human or faerie. I'm a hybrid, a half-breed mix of human and immortal fae, and my veins carry an elixir that holds far greater power than many others. Especially for a hungry vampire. After what happened to my father, I don't want to put myself at risk. There's no one who will come and save me.

I clutch the stake handle, but in the end don't remove it from my belt. The very presence against my palm calms my nerves—at least for now.

He doesn't move. The sun has risen fully and despite the winter season diluting its strength, rays have almost reached his crumpled body.

God damn it.

"At least move to the tree line." I call out the instruction as loudly as my defective voice will allow, but he remains slumped and unmoving, as if already dead. My grip on the stake tightens. "Shit."

I hate vamps. I fucking hate them.

I unsheathe my stake and hold it firmly in my left hand before slamming open the screen door. I stride out onto the porch, watching carefully, but there's still no movement. Nothing at all, until finally I hunch down beside him and dare to poke at his ribs with my weapon.

He lets out a faint groan and one blue eye pops open to stare up at me in weary accusation. "Thought you wanted me dead."

His voice is definitely growing feebler. If he were genuinely trying to trick me, he'd already be up and at my throat. Vamps move fast. Almost as fast as a full-blooded fae. Some of the tension holding my body tight releases just a touch at his continued stillness.

"Yeah," I admit. "I kind of do."

His lids close over the accusatory glare and his wide lips thin slightly. "Then leave me. Just go. It's...probably...for the best, anyway."

His voice is getting weaker by the minute.

I grit my teeth. "That's a stupid thing to say." I roll my eyes at the dramatic behavior. "A martyr-like vampire is ridiculous."

"An oxymoron?"

Despite my wariness, my lips twitch up. "Maybe. And besides, I can't leave you here."

"Why not?" he croaks out.

I notice the sunlight moving at a snail's pace, creeping closer and closer to the vampire. If I linger, I'll be close enough to watch him die. I'll be able to smell his skin as it burns and turns to ash.

I wrinkle my nose as his question settles in me. Why don't I want him dead?

Because I don't want to call in your death. Someone else not far from here died several hours ago, and I don't want to call in anyone else's death today.

"It'd be the wrong thing to do." I say the words with a heaviness I hadn't expected.

"And yet, you carry a stake." His gaze flickers to my weapon before resting back on my face. "Now *that's* kind of oxymoron-ish, don't you think?" Humor laces his response, despite the obvious struggle to speak.

Oh, my God. A comedic vampire. Strange that a creature like this can be in such good humor on the brink of death.

The temptation to grin back at him grows stronger. Only for a second or two, but the lapse shocks me.

"Yeah." I clear my throat, forcing myself to study the grass near his feet. He's more distracting than I expect, and I don't like being at a loss for words. "Funny that. I *will* use it, if I need to. But only in self-defense."

"Fair enough." He nods, one that seems to require a lot of effort on his part.

I don't *want* to discover wit or humor in this creature. I don't want to smile at him, or stare because he's aesthetically pleasing to me. Why am I responding to him in this way? I should let him die. It would merely be one less vamp for others to worry about in the future.

I *feel* death when it comes calling. I feel all the aching sadness of what is about to be, and all the angst and grief of what comes after. Just because my voice is husky and weak, doesn't mean the emotions that well up inside are any less potent. It's the opposite, actually. I can't let any of it out in vocal expression, so everything stays coiled up inside me until there's no room left for anything but the overarching black miasma of death. In those moments, I grow truly afraid that I won't be able to contain the hell inside me, and I'll end up exploding in a splatter of flesh all over the place.

Death, when it comes, is huge and all-encompassing. Sometimes it passes quickly, like it did last night, striking hard and fast and then dispersing as if it never existed at all. At other times, it takes days for that feeling to dissipate. Days for me to start remembering the joy of life, and to start reaching out once again to the light, instead of losing myself in the endless, horrific dark.

Either way, whether hard and fast, or slow and relentless, I won't bring on more death myself. Not even for my worst enemy. Not unless it's a choice between me or them, and this vamp, whoever he is, is not here right now to kill me.

My sigh is long and heartfelt. I cannot believe I'm about to do this. "Just... don't eat me, if I get you inside."

A faint snort of laughter shifts his frame. "I don't eat people. I *drink*. And as to that...I can't promise I won't. I'll try. And I definitely won't drink you dry. But...depends how long it takes to recover."

He won't drink me dry? The honesty that shines through his warped humor is strangely comforting. I probably should be more afraid of him. He just admitted that he'll try not to drink all of me. And yet, tension eases from my shoulders. Even my fingers loosen their grip on the stake.

"Fine." I crouch down next to him and slide my arms under his shoulders. "Just...help me help you. It's not like you're as light as a feather, you know."

I manage to sit him up, but I can't do anything else

without his assistance. I have more strength than a human, but it's not boundless.

It feels...odd, to slide my arm around his muscled frame. For some reason I thought he'd be cold to the touch, and he's not. Though he's not warm either. He's more... room temperature, I suppose.

I shiver at the sensation of being so close to an undead creature. Vamps were the monsters that haunted my childhood. The horror that swept in and took away my family's happiness. I should be running. At least, I should be much more guarded this close to someone like him.

But I am not.

I expect to feel repugnance this close up. Instead, my heart races and strange butterflies beat wildly in my belly as he lifts his good arm to rest across my shoulders and the curve of my body melds effortlessly into his, as if we were made for each other.

I blink. *Made for each other*? Now who is being dramatic? I shake the thought from my head so rapidly I nearly pull a muscle in my neck.

"You all right?" he asks. "Guess it's my turn to check in on you."

"Just, uh, a bee," I say. I refuse to tell him the truth. I'm not sure he believes me, but he doesn't push, which I appreciate.

His scent rises, tempting my nostrils with a heady trace I can't place. Not quite musky, not quite spice. Perhaps something in between? Regardless, it is a little unexpected and very pleasant, indeed. A wave of need sweeps over me so suddenly I stagger.

His grunt brings me back to the task at hand. "Hurts."

"Yeah, okay." I press my lips together. It's only now that I realize how grateful I am that vampires can't read minds. The last thing I need is for this one to use my thoughts against me. "Well, it's bound to hurt, isn't it, with those injuries."

I don't mean to sound so short, but my visceral response to his proximity annoys me.

We fumble our way to a standing position and he leans heavily into me, swaying back and forth before eventually regaining his balance. The long grass scratches at my ankles, adding to the overload on my senses.

"How long before you heal?" I ask, trying to hold onto him in a way that isn't too close but not so loose that he stumbles and falls.

"If I can get out of the sun, a few hours. I think," he adds after a moment. "It's not my first broken bone, but I've never had an arm mangled quite as badly as this. Lucky it's still there at all."

He waves the bitten arm and then sways again, and I support him more firmly around the waist as we lurch up the stairs. Thank goodness for my banshee blood. It provides more strength than if I were merely human. Not as much as a full fae, but some, at least.

Living on a farm, I've gotten used to the silence.

The peace brings a comfort I can't replicate anywhere else. Even the buzzing of flies, the whistle of the wind through the forest canopy and the whisper of breeze-affected leaves all helps relax me. Now, with a vampire in my arms, the silence is thick and cloying rather than peaceful, and something I need to fill before it becomes overwhelming.

"You said there were two attackers?" I say, hoping to keep the conversation going between us.

"Yeah. I've seen it happen before, though not often. Two rogues, working together. It's a concern."

"Because...?" I tilt my head to the side as he takes one step onto the stairs.

A loud squeak pinches the silence. A couple of birds dart off from their branches nearby.

"Because rogues are generally insane and irrational." He says this as though it's a fact, and an obvious one at that. "They don't work with others—they don't have reason enough for that. And they particularly don't collaborate across species. Going rogue seems to exacerbate the underlying discord. Shifters hate vamps, and vice versa. The collaboration, in itself, is a huge red flag. Something's very wrong, and at the present time, whatever it is seems to be centered in this region."

He pauses on the top step and I realize he can't go any further without my say-so. My heart speeds up at what I'm about to do. It goes against everything at my core, but the nearest building is my beekeeping shed where I store all my equipment, and that's one very wide field away from where we're standing. He won't make it that far in daylight. Not with these injuries.

"Fine." I roll my eyes. "You may enter my home."

I cannot believe I'm about to let an actual vampire cross my threshold, but if I leave him out here, exposed to the sun, he'll be dead in a couple of hours, wound or no wound. Last night was truly agonizing. Someone—or something—passed into death not far from here, and I have no wish to inflict that experience on anyone. Even if it is a vampire. Even if maybe they deserve it.

"Do you have a name?" Might as well find out who I'm about to lay out on the couch in my cozy little sitting room.

"Luc Durand."

"French?" That's an interesting piece of information.

"Originally. Many years ago. Before you were born." He emits a faint chuckle. "Probably before your grandparents were born, too."

"Hmm." More jokes. He must think he's cute.

I consider his statement, however. He is probably older than my human grandparents. Not so sure he could make that same claim about the relatives on my mother's side. My banshee blood likely gives me as much longevity as a vamp, if not more. A full fae is immortal.

"Right." I blow out a breath. "We can have a history lesson later. Let's get you lying down then, Lukey."

"Luc." The sharp edge in his correction is clear testament to his dislike of the nickname. This time I let my grin escape as I lead him to my old couch.

"Okie dokie, Lukey."

His answering growl briefly widens my grin, but then he collapses onto the settee and I jump away. Despite logic telling me I'd already be dead if he really wanted to harm me, on some subconscious level I must be still wary. I use the excuse of needing to close the blinds to keep my distance. Without the morning sunlight streaming in, the room darkens, as much as it can during the day, and he lets out a sigh of what sounds like pure relief.

"And yours?" he breathes out.

"Huh?" I turn, arching a brow.

"Your name." He gives me a look. "You do have one, don't you?"

For some reason I'm reluctant. A vague memory surfaces, of a beautiful dark-haired woman leaning over my crib and briefly stroking my cheek. *"Names hold great power, Aleachiarsiwella, particularly for the fair folk. Share yours sparingly, wee child. There are many who would seek to destroy that which they do not understand, and a banshee's blood, even more than our voice, is coveted by many who do not truly understand. In the human realm, you will be known as Aleah and your voice shall be merely a shadow of itself."*

Is that an actual memory, or is it just my mind inventing a mother who stayed around long enough to care, even for a short time? I don't know and that frustrates me more than I wish to admit. I scowl, but Luc continues to wait patiently. There's nothing more disconcerting than trying to outstare a vampire. Their ability to remain unmoving while staring back at you without blinking or breathing is more than most people can take. Vampires are masters at the waiting game.

After a minute, I look away. "Aleah."

I move from the settee and step into the doorway of my kitchen, deciding to put distance between the two of us and busy myself with something other than staring at him.

"Pretty."

"Uh huh." I nod enthusiastically. *And easier to say than the real one.*

"Almost as pretty as your long, dark hair." His eyes linger on my hair and I have to flex my fingers to keep myself from brushing said hair back over my shoulder.

I ignore the belly flutter his compliment re-ignites.

"Okay, Luc." This time I avoid the silly nickname. "What do you need? Anything to...um..."

I trail off awkwardly, glancing around the kitchen for help. I nearly said drink, but the only suitable drink in this place right now would be me. And my two cats, but they're already out for their morning ablutions somewhere, and I'm damn sure not letting them back inside while this visitor is in residence.

"I fed recently, Aleah, so you're not at risk," he says,

and for some reason I believe him. "Despite the delectable scent of your blood."

My heart jolts, but his eyelids are starting to droop.

"I won't need...*that*...for at least a couple of days. Just sleep. Out of the sun, my body will heal itself, eventually."

He releases an enormous yawn and for the first time I catch sight of his fangs. They're sheathed, but even so, the pointy white ends transform him instantly from handsome man to sexy predator. He yawns again. I should look anywhere except at him, but I can't help it. I stare, definitely longer than necessary. I'm glad he doesn't seem to notice.

Without any further warning, he immediately drops into a state completely and utterly immobile. He looks dead. Pale, unmoving, and not breathing. I stagger back, almost afraid to do anything. I know I didn't cause this, but it's still unnerving. Of course, he's not dead, not exactly. He's *undead*. The distinction makes quite a difference when you're a banshee. It's still alarming to observe the phenomenon as closely as this.

I'm tempted to creep up and have an even more thorough look, but vamps are tricky and you never know when one will decide you're their next dinner. Especially after his comment about the scent of my blood. If I had a long enough stick, I may have poked him, just to be sure he isn't a threat presently, although that might have riled him up.

I hadn't realized he'd clocked my blood's scent. Clearly, he knows I'm fae, or to be more accurate, part fae. He probably doesn't know what kind, yet, as there are few banshees now left in this realm. My mother is apparently one of the last of her kind, at least according to my aunt. After mating with my father and staying long enough to give birth to me, she said goodbye and simply walked out one day without ever looking back. My dad's sister, who raised me after Dad passed away, called her a banshee witch and said she was on a mission to create more of her kind. If that's true, I expect I have several half-siblings by now, somewhere out there in the wider world.

I suppose I should be curious about any so-called fae family. The truth is, since my father's passing, I've tried to embrace my normal "human" half as much as I possibly can in the circumstances. My aunt was never hugely loving toward me, but at least she was there when I needed her. She's the one who confirmed the details of what happened to my dad, and taught me that vampires are evil. I've managed to live a mostly normal human existence over the years, except for those times when death swoops in and almost destroys me with the agony. Sometimes, out here in the woods on my isolated property, I forget that I'm anything other than human.

Or at least I did, until someone died last night, and then a certain injured vampire rocked up on my doorstep and stared at me with sexy hunger deep within his gaze. *Coincidence*? I don't believe it is, and yet still, my body instantly responded with an answering primal call. It is as if his arrival heralded my awakening from a long hibernation. A physical awakening, and one I neither need, nor want.

After a few minutes of awkwardly standing still in the doorway of the room, I realize the stupidity of continuing in this vein. I sidle across to the armchair opposite the couch and take a seat. No way am I leaving him alone to wake up and snoop around, or jump out and attack me when I'm least expecting it. But there's no reason I can't be comfortable while I'm waiting. It *is* my own home, after all.

I allow myself a moment to rest my head back against the chair and close my eyes. I can't fully relax, not with the threat of attack so close by, but I can get off my feet and let my body rest. It has been a trying twenty-four hours, livelier than I'm used to.

I can't help but wonder about the vampire now in my home—Luc. Where did he come from? Why is he here in this quiet, rural part of the world, and how did he get so badly injured that he needed to ask for help? Who exactly was he hunting? Why would a supe go rogue and be threatening this region in particular? There's nothing in Hatton Grove but honest farm folk and a typical Australian rural community.

A rogue in this area is rare. It's unthinkable. Two at the same time is almost unheard of, in my admittedly limited experience. It's enough to raise the alert.

Am I—or my few very human friends and neighbors—in danger, either from this vampire, or the crazed supes he says he's hunting? What are they doing here anyway? What is so special about farmland?

I live out of the city for a reason. Carnivorous creatures tend to congregate near the habitat of their prey, and here in the country, far from crowds, it's rare to see preternaturals like vamps or shifters, other than those briefly passing through on their way to a larger town or city.

Being around other supes makes me uncomfortable. It is a reminder that I'm just as supernatural as I am human, and I haven't really come to terms with the fact that I am part-banshee. It's not like I'm in denial of what I am, but I don't want to broadcast it, either. Since supes have a talent of being able to sense others like them, being away from them makes sense.

I *like* my solitary life out here on my small farm acreage. The local township is several miles away and the nearest human family is a mile away, over the hills. I like that the only living things near me are my cats, my beloved bees, and the local wildlife inhabiting the nearby forest. I like the quiet. I like knowing I won't be bothered and I won't be discovered for what I really am.

The distance limits exposure to the banshee wail. Being alone is far safer. For me, and for those I care about.

Hearing a banshee in full cry is one of the most chilling things a human can experience—or so I was told by my aunt. "Trouble follows you, Aleah," she used to say. "Trouble and terror, in equal measure."

If there's an underlying ache of loneliness at living such a secluded life, that ache is nothing compared to the pain of death when it comes calling.

For years I thought dad's death was my fault. My banshee side that recognizes and calls to death, had somehow brought it upon *him*. And now, death has come calling once again, and a vampire is asleep in my living room. Is the trouble and terror about to escalate, or has it already arrived?

Chapter Two

LUC

The delicious perfume of honey surrounds her. I noticed it briefly when she assisted me into her home, but now she must be leaning directly over me, as the heady scent has intensified ten-fold. I'm tempted to take just a nibble, to see if she tastes as delicious as she smells.

I won't.

But I want to.

I open my eyes and, sure enough, meet her suddenly startled gaze only a few inches from my own face. Her irises are a delightful shade of hazel that shifts from gray-green to brown and back again, depending on the moment. I've never seen eyes like hers before. I can't help but stare.

It's hard to pinpoint their color, actually. It changes seemingly at whim, but whatever their truth, her eyes are a perfect match for the cascading dark-brown hair falling in waves across her shoulders and down. My fingers itch to tangle in that glorious hair.

"Oh!" She jumps back, as if afraid I'll lurch up and have her for dinner.

Her fingers spasm at her side and this time I wonder if she'll unsheathe that ridiculous wooden stake. How long has she been carrying it around, thinking it provides her with any real safety? The spindly end wouldn't even make it through my layers of clothing, let alone penetrate my skin or drill deep enough to pierce my heart.

I cock my head to the side, taking in her hand, her long fingers. Despite the feminine length, I know she's more than just a pretty face. For her to be here, by herself, means she has to know how to handle the land. If she didn't, she wouldn't be able to survive. I wonder if she crafted the stake herself, or if she purchased it from someone using fear to make a buck.

I consider snatching it off her and snapping it in half, but that would be rude. She has shown kindness in providing shelter when that action is clearly against her instinct. The last thing I want is to have her question her kindness. I don't want to be the reason she doesn't offer it again.

Instead, I take a deep breath and suck air into my lungs, not because I need to, but because sometimes it just feels good. It's a reminder of what it was like to be alive. And at this moment, it provides a way to draw her enticing scent all the way down to the center of my being.

My cock stirs and I have to concentrate to keep my body in check. It has been a long time since I felt the rush of desire as keenly as I did when I first caught Aleah's scent. It's almost embarrassing how much I want her, and it takes great effort to keep myself restrained.

"Sorry," she says in a voice husky with what sounds like embarrassment. Her hand goes to her hair and begins to fuss with the long locks. The movement fascinates me. "You weren't breathing. It's been hours, and I couldn't tell if you were...well...*actually* dead."

"I am." I sit up and test my arm and shoulder. I can't continue to look at that hair or the way she's running her fingers through it. If I do, I'll reach out and do the same thing, and that's the last thing either of us needs.

My injury is much better. Almost completely healed and only a small residue of pain and scarring left over the crush wound where the werewolf's jaws caught me unexpectedly. I must have slept for longer than I planned. A glance toward the window shows the blind now raised and the gray of early evening already draping the sky. More than a few hours, then. I must have been out for the count for almost the whole day.

"You're not, though. Dead, I mean." Her voice is still low, and I realize it's not embarrassment fueling the huskiness. It must just be the way she speaks. The rasp is rather sexy, but without my refined hearing ability I doubt I could pick up all her words.

"Sorry to disappoint you, but you do know I'm a vamp—"

"Of course, I know *that*." Acid colors her tone. "But you're *undead*, not dead. There's a difference. *I* should know." She bristles, crossing her arms over her chest.

The penny drops and curiosity blooms as I realize what kind of fae has invited me into her home. I narrow my eyes. "You're a banshee."

One of the rarest and most misunderstood of all the fae. Some say they're not strictly fae at all. Many are afraid of the banshee cry, which purportedly means death for those who hear it. From all accounts there are very few left in the world today, and those still here are making noises about returning forever to the fae realm. Is Aleah one of those fair folk who eventually plans to forsake the mortal world?

Her arms wrap even tighter across her chest and she looks away. I'm not sure she's going to answer when she finally mutters, "Half."

"Ah." A hybrid. Lucky for her I fed last night, or I'd be all over that delectable neck in a heartbeat. *Her* heartbeat. Hybrid blood is the most delicious aphrodisiac known to my kind.

I'm surprised she admitted such a thing. She clearly doesn't trust me—and for good reason. I don't hold her caution against her. This isn't the typical environment for supes—which is probably why she chose this dwelling in the first place. But the fact that she's a half-breed puts her even more at risk. From supes. And definitely from me.

No wonder my loins are stirring so vigorously. It's her blood, calling to mine. Nothing more, nothing less. Pure lust, fueled by the desire to feast on a hybrid human-fae.

My trousers tighten further across my groin. Her gaze drops only briefly but the instant flush of color in her cheeks is telling. I should hide my desire for her. I should probably have a little more shame.

But I don't.

If anything, I'm curious to know how she'll respond.

I lean back, letting my thighs drop open a little wider both to ease my own discomfort and add to hers. *Do you like what you see, Aleah?* Fae are notoriously sexual beings, but little Miss Half-and-half, here, is acting as if she has never even seen a member of the opposite sex, let alone enjoyed the carnal delights both our species often celebrate.

She turns away, and then back again as if she has gotten herself under control. The flush in her cheeks is gone, but that glorious pulse at the base of her throat beats faster than it did a minute ago. I eye that beat, enjoying its tempo and imagining the flavor of her blood. Would it taste like honey? Or something even sweeter, perhaps?

"I'd offer you something to drink, but..."

She shrugs and for the first time the hint of a smile that seems entirely genuine graces her lips. Only for a moment, but it's enough that I want to see it again.

"What?" she asks, as though something is wrong.

I blink. I don't realize at first that I'm staring at her lips. When I do, I force my gaze upward to focus on her eyes instead.

"Nothing," I say. "It's just..."

"Yes?"

"I didn't realize banshees had the capacity to make jokes."

She rolls her eyes, making no move to hide the obvious exasperation.

I close my legs. Baiting her seems petty, and the moment for teasing is past. "You'll be safe for another day or so, and by then I'll be long gone."

My body is back under control and I no longer have the urge to unsheathe my incisors. At least, that's what I tell myself. I stifle a heartfelt growl at the residual ache in my groin.

"I need to report in to my department." I rise to my feet and reach for her hand.

As quick as my movement is, hers is quicker. Her fist clutches the stake so tightly her knuckles turn white. She wields the poor excuse for a weapon in front of her.

Those beautiful eyes are narrowed and no longer soft and mysterious.

"Stay back," she commands, her voice firm.

"I merely wished to thank you for your assistance." I raise up my hands in defense. "You saved my life this morning, Aleah. Or did you forget?"

"Oh. Okay." Slowly, she lowers the weapon.

I strike with my kind's natural speed, seizing her wrist and twisting hard to force her to drop the piece of wood.

She releases a soft shriek that is stifled before it can fully form. I pull her close, wrapping one arm around her waist and raising her imprisoned hand to my mouth.

"I meant it, Aleah." I hope she can detect the sincerity in my tone. It's important she understands. Under normal circumstances, I wouldn't care, but for some reason she makes things feel different. "This is merely a thank you."

When my lips graze her skin, I taste honey and sunlight, and all things bright and warm. It's unexpected in a banshee. In fact, everything about Aleah is unexpected. The only one of her kind I've come across in the past may have been a dark-haired beauty like this one, but was full of bitterness and sorrow and lost regret.

Perhaps the human aspect of her blood provides hope, where normally such an emotion would not reside?

I flip her hand until it is palm up and only a couple of inches from my lips. Her radial artery pulses fast and strong. *Life force. Lifeblood.* The rush of adrenalin is instant, causing my fangs to unsheathe and the flesh between my legs to harden once again.

So much for remaining in control.

I almost feel silly. I shouldn't let something as inconsequential as lust make my body do things without permission. It reminds me of how I used to act when I was first turned, more animal than human, searching for a way to satiate the most basic needs of food and sex.

Her intake of breath is sharp. I can't tell if fear or desire drives her to wriggle within my firm hold, but the action only serves to entice my flesh to full erection.

"Stop moving, little banshee, unless…" *Unless you're ready to sink your sweet body onto my hungry cock and let craving take us beyond thought into another state of being altogether.*

I don't need to complete the warning. Her body stills instantly, a delightful pink flush spreading out across her cheeks.

There's an inner war playing out within her changeable eyes. It's obvious that she craves me in return, and yet the craving clearly horrifies her. Delight and revulsion combat. Which emotion will win out? Her small white teeth—so neat and even and nothing like my pointed fangs—worry at her plump bottom lip. Plump, pink, *blood-filled* lips. I want to taste those lips.

"Don't." She shakes her head, correctly interpreting

my thought process. A delicate shiver trembles through her body still pinned against mine. "You *promised*."

Forget lips. I want to taste every delicious inch of this creature. The need grows and I can't help myself. Her wrist is still only an inch from my hungry fangs. I flick out my tongue and lick the radial pulse, enjoying the crazy beat. It seems to jump at my touch. My cock twitches at the way she's affected. Because of me. *Heaven.*

Her scent—indeed, her lifeblood—rushes through that vein in pulsing waves. Only the barest membrane separates my mouth from the ambrosia on tap beneath her skin. All I need to do is pierce her skin with the tip of my fang. It could be over in less than a second. It could be so quick, she wouldn't even realize what was happening.

Her life force. Mine.

The pull is almost too powerful to resist. I graze her wrist with the tip of a fang and prepare to breach. A slow, purring growl erupts from my chest in anticipation of the rush.

She tries to yank away her hand.

"No!" I tighten my hold. "Do. Not. Move."

Her rapid breath hitches and then stops altogether. Silence reigns as I wrestle against my nature. Hybrid blood to a vampire is like crack to an addict. *Impossible to resist. Impossible...* Precious seconds tick away, until finally, somehow, I find the strength to twist my head to one side and release us both from our stasis.

Her breathing recommences more unevenly than before, as if she's aware of just how close I came to taking her blood. That danger is receding but could re-emerge at any second, and by her wary narrow-eyed look, she knows it, too.

"I didn't promise, actually." I aim for levity but it is clear that neither of us are quite ready. "To set the record straight, I said I'd try. But I believe it may be safe for you to move now."

I retract my fangs, giving truth to the words, and let her hand drop. I expect her to jump away from someone she probably sees as a rabid monster. *What possessed me*? Like most vampires since the Accord, I never take blood without first gaining permission. There are any number of vampire groupies around—even in a rural location like Hatton Grove—who will throw themselves at my kind. The taking of blood is closely connected to the sexual experience. It can heighten the sensation of lovemaking for both giver and taker, and most humans will never experience an orgasm as intense as the one a vampire will deliver for them during sex.

Aleah seems like the antithesis of a vamp groupie. I wait for the inevitable recoil and yet, for some reason, her body remains pressed close against mine. *Why?*

I'm surprised by how difficult it is just moving away from her. Not only because she's a hybrid, but it feels like something else, something I can't quite put my finger on.

Tentatively, I raise my hands and grip her loosely around the hips. Still she doesn't pull away. I become aware of many things all at once. The slightness of her build despite her height, which is extraordinary; she pretty much single-handedly carried me inside early this morning. The bemused look in her eyes that are once again soft and dreamy, their hazel depths encouraging a deep dive within to discover more of her mysterious soul. The enticing warmth of her thighs against mine that offer a silent invitation for so much more.

My erection reforms for a third time, the softness of her lower belly juxtaposing beautifully against the firm ridge of my flesh. I may have been able to sheathe my fangs, at least temporarily, but my cock refuses to comply. I should be able to command it the same way I do every other part of my body, but Aleah makes it so easy for me to lose control. And I'm in no rush to regain it.

Her mouth is half parted, the tip of her tongue darting out to moisten her lips. My eyes are drawn to them and I muffle a slight moan. *So luscious.*

Is she doing this on purpose? She's calling out to be kissed, even if she won't admit that thought consciously. I push a loose tendril of hair off her cheek and lean in, testing her reaction. A quick shake of her head provides one message, while the heat between her legs intensifies. I know, because her mound is nicely sandwiched against the base of my cock and that heat sends an altogether different message.

"Mixed communication, little banshee," I murmur against her mouth.

She doesn't pull away. Instead, her panting breath warms my lips. I secure her more tightly, cradling her butt cheeks in my palms and using my strength to hold her in place. Pressure centers fully in my groin and my balls tighten in anticipation of imminent coupling.

"Which is it, Aleah? Do I stay, or do I leave?"

"I don't understand this." Her voice is deliciously raspy, more so than it has been thus far. Her eyes darken from a golden color to molten bronze, like melting caramel. She can pretend all she wants, but her body gives away her need. "Are you...hypnotizing me, or something?"

"Hypnotizing?" My laugh is brief, but intense. "You've been watching too much television. I can influence humans, up to a point. But no vampire can influence a fae. Yes, the lure of a vampire to a hybrid is almost as strong as the reverse, but it's a purely physical lure with no mind-fuck involved. I seriously doubt I could influence you to do anything you don't wish to do, half-fae or not. This decision is all on you. If you want me to leave, then say so now."

"No, I..." She closes her eyes for a moment, then opens them and meets my gaze squarely. Surprisingly, the confusion remains. She shifts her weight and my cock responds.

I press my lips together to keep a groan from releasing. I need her to be sure about this. It won't be as good if she thinks I'm manipulating her into wanting sex with me.

"I don't *know* what I want," she says. "I hate vampires. I've always hated them."

Hmm. Nothing ambiguous about that. Why does she hate my kind so relentlessly?

I'm about to ask her when she continues to speak.

"But I can't seem to say no to wanting you to stay."

"Of course, you can't." My grin is smug. "And why would you want to? I am known for my prowess in the bedroom. And right this minute...Aleah, I need to taste—"

"*No blood!*" she shrieks. Her fingers curl into tight fists. I get the impression she may even try to retrieve her discarded stake, even if it won't do me any harm.

Her cry is sharp, almost fury-driven, and my incisors unsheathe in response as a hiss leaves my lips.

"You certainly don't make it easy, do you?" I draw in a deep breath and let it out slowly, allowing time to regain a modicum of calm. "If I cannot sample your delectable blood, then I *will* have your lips."

I make good on my promise before she changes her mind yet again, crushing her mouth beneath mine. There is more ferocity in the action than I plan, but her unintentional tease annoys me, especially when my own blood is already up and calling for plunder. When a tiny moan vibrates up from her throat, a bolt of desire tightens my loins further.

She tastes exactly as I imagined she would, all honey and flowers and innocence. Her sweetness soothes the darkness within me in a way that hasn't happened in the whole of my life as a vampire. I want to devour her, and yet there's something holding me in check. After a minute, I soften the onslaught to cajole, rather than bully a response.

When she finally capitulates and begins kissing me back, it feels like a triumph far greater than merely winning someone over with persuasion. In that capitulation I'm reminded of what it's like to be alive. What it's like to have a heart that beats so fast and so powerfully that you wonder if it's going to jump right out of your chest at the force of emotion running through you.

Emotion? What is she doing to me? Why am I drawn to her so strongly, when it's obvious she can't wait to get me out of her home and out of her life for good? Is this attraction merely the enticing promise of hybrid blood, or is it based on something more?

I nearly pull away. This emotion she's making me feel is unfamiliar and unnerving and I don't like it. And yet, I can't untangle myself from her body. I can't rid myself of her inviting warmth, even amidst all of her confusion.

I don't know anything about Aleah, beyond her

species and her name, and she knows nothing about me. Yet this kiss runs like fire along my veins, in a potent rush that feels more real than the taking of blood ever did in the past. I crave even more of it.

When at last we break apart, she is panting loudly and her previously pale cheeks are flushed a delicate pink again. I don't *need* to breathe to survive, but in the aftermath of this kiss even I am drawing breath once again, albeit with a slight rasp that sounds rusty from misuse.

"That was...very intense." My brain feels fuzzy and disconnected from reason. The warm pliancy of her mouth beneath mine is still all-consuming in my thoughts. *I want to fuck her. I* need *to fuck her.* It will be amazing, to seduce this beautiful woman whose scent and taste reminds me of life, and the joy of living.

And once I have her screaming my name, I will sink my teeth in her flesh and I will taste her. I will claim her as mine, and she will writhe beneath me and beg me to do it again and again. "Shall we go to your bedr—"

Her eyes spring open. "No!"

"But—"

"I rescind my invitation," she says, her voice strong, her eyes fierce. "I changed my mind, Luc. You are no longer welcome in my home."

What the hell?

"I—" My legs begin to shuffle of their own accord

toward the door. I scowl as I twist to stare back at her, even while moving away. "You can't be serious. Why—"

"You're a *vampire*." Her lips are swollen from our kiss and she rubs at them with the back of her hand as if trying to wipe away the taste of me. "I won't have you in my home a moment longer than absolutely necessary. I thought I could—but I can't. I *can't*. I don't understand what you're doing to me, why I'm reacting like this, but I refuse to participate in it anymore. I won't risk it." Tears shimmer in her eyes, turning them emerald.

"But—"

"It would be a betrayal."

"Of whom?" I reach out to the door and turn the handle, with no control over my own limbs until I'm standing outside on the top step of the porch. The gray of evening has intensified, and even though it's not yet dead of night when I'm at full strength, there's no sun left in the day to pose a threat any longer. "The only one I see you betraying here is yourself."

She shakes her head, but without conviction.

"Don't deny yourself." I try one last time. "Don't lie to yourself. You can pretend to send me away because of what I am, but we both know that isn't true."

She glares at me. It only makes me more determined than ever to try and get through to her.

"Why, Aleah? You knew what I was when you invited me in. I didn't hurt you. And you want it as much as I do."

She follows me to the doorway and stares out with big, haunted-looking eyes. To anyone human, she'd be a gray silhouette in the darkness, but I see through the shadows better than any other creature bar demons, and I read the angst and sorrow in her features. I know I'm right. What's more, she knows I'm right as well.

She looks away, her bottom lip jutted out into a pout. "I'm sorry, Luc."

"What are you afraid of?"

The rejection is unfamiliar. Since being turned almost two hundred and fifty years ago, I've had my pick of lovers, men and women alike, and no one has ever said no to my advances. *Not a single one.* I don't understand this. Why deny herself the pleasure she knows she'll receive? Why banish me before I can prove myself to her?

"It's clear that you're conflicted," I say, "but I thought you'd made up your mind."

"I'm not afraid, and I'm *not* conflicted." She folds her arms across her chest, but this time I see the gesture more as a mechanism of self-defense than anything to do with anger. She's afraid I'll penetrate through her walls, even more than I already have. "I want nothing to do with vampires. *Nothing.* And I especially don't want one in my bed."

Her cheeks are deeply stained with color. It makes her look even more becoming. I can't take my eyes off of her.

"Liar."

I breathe the word, almost under my breath, but her slight start proves that she hears me. *Of course, she does.* The fae portion of her blood boosts her sensory ability more than that of a purely mortal woman.

She closes her eyes, chewing her bottom lip. It seems as though she's debating within herself. Finally, she looks at me, almost helpless.

"A vampire ruined my life once," she says. "I won't let it happen again."

Silence falls in the night air. *A vampire ruined her life?*

I consider whether to press for details, but the desperate conviction in her gaze convinces me it would be futile. She won't tell me anything. I'm surprised by how disappointed I am when I realize this.

After a moment, I let it go, and nod once. "Our story is not done, little banshee. I will be back, and then? We *will* talk."

Her answer is a slammed door. I'm left standing in the dark on my own, as a light drizzle begins to fall. There's a real chill in the air without the sun, but that suits me just fine. I barely feel the elements anymore. Being undead has its perks. The bird chatter eventually quiets down and the night creatures begin to stir.

Night creatures like me. Night creatures like the two who tag-teamed their assault, one crushing my arm in his jaws as I fought to retrieve the child he had taken to feed on, while the other circled, waiting for the right moment to attack.

My thoughts reluctantly turn back to business as I move away from Aleah's cottage toward the forest.

It amazes me how easily distracted from my work I've become simply being around Aleah for a few hours. I shake my head, needing focus. It is especially important to keep my concentration with the threat of the two preternaturals still out and about.

There was something off about those two, even more than their clearly loco state. Perhaps I'm overreacting and it was simply the insane light behind their eyes, or the unexpected strength beyond even what one might expect from a rogue fueled by madness. I don't understand what was driving them, but it is rare for any shifter to get the advantage over a vampire with as much experience as me. Even more rare, to find two insane rogues of opposing species working in tandem.

And there was something more. Something inherently *wrong* that I can't quite pinpoint, beyond an instinctive gut feeling that they smelled...*bad.*

Evil.

I've seen too much in the past couple of centuries to frighten easily, but that sense of something malevolent and calculating is new, and off-the-charts worrying.

In the thirtyish years since the Accord Agreement was reached—an agreement that all signing parties, human and non-human alike, promised to abide by—investigative units were set up to ensure compliance. Units like the one I work for.

The rules of the Accord are clear. All are to obey the new laws and respect life wherever possible. Innocents are untouchable. On the matter of humans, everyone is in agreement. Adults are a last resort, and children are strictly off the menu. This is the way it's supposed to be.

In a world where preternaturals have finally emerged from the shadows, the new rules allow us to co-exist with each other and with humans, if not peacefully, at least with some semblance of order.

The only exception to the Accord is the celestials. Angels and demons. No one has ever been able to convince them to cooperate, but there are hunters and negotiators who specialize in that area, while the rest of us try to steer clear.

The witches, and fae, and various minor non-human species, all signed the Accord alongside humans. Shifters these days usually make do with deer, or maybe cattle, sheep, or rabbits when they hunt. Depends on their shifter breed, of course, as to what size prey they choose to bring down.

Vamp cooperation varies greatly, depending on their House. Some Masters and Mistresses, like mine until she met her final destruction a quarter century ago, have been willing to adopt the tenets of the Accord, at least on the surface. There are others who still choose to live outside the laws of this world, and it is now my job to ensure those transgressors are caught and appropriately sanctioned. Appropriate sanctions usually mean death. Units like mine are the only ones allowed to enforce the law in such a way. Especially when the goal is to save an innocent life.

Like the child I was unable to save last night.

To take a child... a small boy who did nothing more than respond to the cry of what probably sounded like a stray animal and wander out into the garden looking for it...

Rage rises at the thought of the monster who got away. I bite my bottom lip in order to keep myself from revealing a telling growl. Harming innocents is not something that sits well with me, regardless of what sort of species they are.

Together, the rogues may have managed to crush my body, but I took the lifeblood of at least one of the fuckers. Too late for the child, sadly, but at least I know that particular shifter will never again take a human prey. His vamp partner, on the other hand, is another matter altogether. He's still out there, and I'm positive he will attack again. Whether he does so alone or finds another partner is moot. He seeks death and destruction, and it makes me unsettled, knowing something like that is on the hunt.

Once, years ago in the much larger city of Melbourne to the south, something similar happened after the Accord was initially struck. Many innocent people died before the culprits were stopped and the Accord investigative units fully came into their power.

No one ever figured out why or how two loups could work together back then.

Rogues are normally loners who will kill without mercy or remorse until someone brings them down. The fact that two of them appeared to be working together in this instance, is far more concerning than I let on to Aleah. I need to contact the department's head office and let them know this is more than a simple case of a lone loco wolf or a blood-mad vamp.

As a detective in the new order, it's my job to keep the peace, and I've sworn an oath to that end. I need to find the other one—this killer rogue—and keep him alive long enough to find out what the fuck is going on.

It's probably a good thing Aleah rejected me. If I stayed and tangled myself with her, who knows how long I would have been distracted. If I had tasted her...

My loins stir, but I force the feeling away. I have a job to do, and thinking about Aleah and all the ways I could have brought her to her knees is not something that will help uncover what is going on here and stop more needless death.

From the edge of the forest, I cast one last look at Aleah's cozy little cottage in which all the lights inside blaze. I know it's a deliberate action from her. A message to me that she's inside bathed in light, while I'm back out here in the damp darkness where I belong. A message that tells me to stay away, to stay in the darkness.

Doesn't matter. I'm a vampire. I *do* belong in the darkness.

Sexy little banshee. Regardless of her cold behaviour, I meant what I said. I *will* return, and when I do, I'm going to prove her wrong about vampires. We might belong to the night, but we're not all diseased, blood-sucking monsters who kill without discretion or mercy. We can inflict pleasure just as easily as pain. We can create feelings of bliss and elation just as well as fear. I can show her that.

The thought of how I might prove that to Aleah is strangely exhilarating, even as I slink away into the night to continue my search for a loup who likely epitomizes exactly the type of insane and rabid monster she's afraid of.

The thought of Aleah is added motivation to solve this quickly. Then I can return and show her just what being a vampire actually means. I can introduce the banshee to the lustful pleasures of sexual fulfilment with a vamp in the prime of his undead life.

Chapter Three

ALEAH

I cannot *believe* I let him do that. My face heats with embarrassment, with absolute and utter shame at my atrocious behavior. I could rant and rave all night about not having any choice in the matter, but it wouldn't be true. Of *course*, I had a choice. I could have rescinded my invitation at any time.

Instead, for some weird reason, I chose to let him kiss me. What's worse is I actually liked it. I wanted him to kiss me again. It was why I couldn't bring myself to push him away at first. At least I had the strength to say no before it went much further.

Too bad my body doesn't feel as happy as my head about the fact that he left. Too bad the zing in my woman bits is still making itself felt, even though he's out there in the dark somewhere and no longer pressing his engorged and very ready organ against my aching and equally ready clit.

Holy motherfucking hell. I almost let him drink my blood.

That's what scares me the most. The fact that I know better and yet it made no difference. I wanted him enough to put my values—and myself—at risk.

There is something about Luc that forces down my guard and makes me forget who or what he is, without even realizing that it's happening. Is that how vamps lure their prey? With charm and sexual chemistry? Making sure their victim switches off the logical and thinking part of themselves and, instead, switches on their rampaging libido? He says he can't control my mind because I'm part-fae, but I'm not sure I believe him. Would I have been so open about wanting him, otherwise? Incapable of important things like movement and breathing?

Despite the fact that, up until today, I've harbored nothing but hatred for all things vampiric, it seems one particular vamp has definitely managed to get under my skin in a most unexpected way. Am I this easy to push over? Would this have happened with any other vampire?

I simply don't know. And that thought scares me even more.

I'm glad he's out of my house. I'm glad he disappeared so quickly and seemingly without care. Back in the dark where you belong, monster.

The thoughts might be fierce, but they feel hollow. *Was my aunt wrong all these years? Is it possible there are good as well as evil vampires? Just like there are with any other species?*

I hurry around the house, switching on all the overhead lights. It's a stupid gesture but I can't seem to stop until the whole cottage is lit up like a Christmas tree. My heart races. Every now and then, I can't help but glance at the door to see if he'll try to get back in.

He can't, I remind myself. *I have to invite him in and I won't do that.*

And yet, I still worry. Almost like I don't trust myself.

Will I ever see him again? Do I want *to see him again?* I can't settle at anything, and I'm grateful when Bobo and Suki appear out of nowhere, scratching at the door and demanding their dinner. My two Siamese cats are nothing if not predictable, especially when it comes to their stomachs. Dodging their sinuous bodies as they wind in and out around my legs gives me something other than a sexy vampire to think about.

I'm relieved to know they're back inside, away from the loup danger that I'm disturbed to hear lurks outside. I'm positive my cats are able to take care of themselves but I'm glad to see they're safe.

Once the fur babies have been fed, I add a frozen curry to the microwave for myself. I might even have a glass of wine tonight, to celebrate. To celebrate what? Who the hell knows, but I feel like a glass of *something*, so I pull out a bottle of white wine from the refrigerator. I run my thumb over the label. I don't know enough about wine to care about the date or where it's from. Hopefully it will taste good.

I'm just about to crack it open when pain and darkness rolls over me like a wave that threatens to drown me. *Death and dying.* Oh, God. Another attack.

One moment life is completely normal, and the next the wine bottle smashes all over the floor. The cats screech and flee to the next room. I bend double, clutching at my belly as a rising wail pushes its way inexorably upward out of my chest.

No, no, no, no...

Not now. Not again. Two nights in a row. I can't do this!

Who is it? Can I get there in time to warn them? Oh, my God!

Agony rips at my belly, causing me to hunch over. My fingers spasm and my breath sounds become harsh as I fight to remain on my feet. Light flashes my vision. I see stars. My head starts to spin, to throb. It's hard to retain my balance.

It has to be someone close by. Much closer than last night. My range as a half-human is more restricted than a full-blood banshee, which is why I moved so far out of the city. Fewer people. Less death. Less of this agonizing need to wail so loud that the whole world can hear my warning.

Only, no one *ever* hears my wail. *Defective... fucking...voice.*

Unbearable. I have to let it out.

Somehow, I manage to stagger outside and down

the porch stairs. I make it all the way across my front garden before the next wave hits. The perfume from my gorgeous winter flowers laced with recent rain permeates the air, and I suck in deep breaths, fighting the call of death and focusing on the fresh scent of life and growth.

Not death. Not tonight. Not if I can help it.

Another surge of pain rushes through me and I clutch at the garden gate, fighting the wail. *I have to get there in time. I have to let them know.*

When the crescendo of pain briefly retreats, I wrench open the gate that separates my yard from the paddocks, and make my way across one of the grassy fields that make up the remainder of my property. If anyone is watching—unlikely in this rural setting—I must look like a drunken fool, lurching and staggering, falling in the long damp grass and rising, as the pain takes hold more fully and death becomes ever more certain.

Finally, I reach the gate on the other side that leads from my land to the neighboring property. I can smell the sweet nectar, a familiar scent that wraps around me like a warm blanket. My beehives are off somewhere to the left, hidden in the darkness. *My beautiful honey bees. I hope you're safe. I hope you're sleeping.*

The trees thin out at this point and I totter through the gate into an open meadow where my view down the hill into the valley is uninterrupted. The windows are ablaze with light in the farmhouse at the base of the incline.

My closest neighbors, Darrie and Gwen, have lived here for a long time. Darrie's family has owned this land for generations. Despite my preference for isolation, they always check in on me at least once a week with homemade apple pie. In exchange, they take home a jar of my honey. *No. Not them. Please, not them.* I have very few friends in this world, and those I have allowed to sneak in under my emotional guard are very special people, indeed.

The wail is imminent. I fight it. I fight it so hard, until I can't fight it one second longer. The sound bursts forth from my throat in a blast of fae-touched energy. If I were a full banshee the whole region would hear my keening. Maybe if I were, someone might come to assist the person in need.

But I am not full-fae. And no one comes.

Instead, all that permeates the air is muted sobbing. My voice is defective, my wail all but useless, and just as I failed my beloved father all those years ago, I'm about to fail Darrie or Gwen.

I fail all of them. Every time. I'm never, ever enough. And yet, I cannot stop this mangled wail from coming, and I cannot make it greater than what it already is. I am useless.

Nausea rises and I drop to my knees. I'm not going to reach them in time to warn them.

I start to crawl, my hands and knees squelching in dirt made damp by recent drizzle.

Don't die. Please don't die. Let me be wrong this time. Please let me be wrong.

Nothing ever seems to protect the innocent from the various evils that stalk the earth. Regardless, all I can do is utter a prayer of hope, of pleading for the opportunity to finally do something.

I can't. The moment death arrives, I give up the futile crawl and curl into a tight ball, keening in near silence, unable to move further as waves of nausea from the agony of death wash over me like relentless surf against a rocky shore.

I am a pathetic ball of uselessness. I cannot help and I cannot get others to hear me. What good am I? Death is imminent and I can't help those who need it.

Which of them has been taken? Why? And how? If there was anything I *could* do, I would do it, but I already know I'm too late. Instead I just lay here in the grass in Darrie's home paddock, sniffling amidst the wet earth and the cow patties and living the reality of death. *So much death.*

I stare up at the sky above me. Tiny pinprick stars light up the black sky, and I feel myself burn with anger. Why is the backdrop against such tragedy so beautiful? The contrast makes me retch, and I roll onto my knees, preparing myself for the oncoming vomit. I heave once, twice, but nothing comes.

The agony goes on, longer and more intense than ever before, and my keening intensifies in nature. *Oh, no. More than one.* This time, there must be more than one death.

I can't bear the thought of losing either, but both? Unthinkable. Darrie and Gwen are an older couple who opened their home and their hearts to me, a strange and lonely young woman, when I first arrived in the region. I boarded with them for two years, until they transferred the mostly wooded portion of their land atop the hill and presented the title to me as a gift. They gave me everything I now own, simply because of their innate kindness. I owe my *life* to them. I owe my continuing connection with humanity to this beautiful and generous couple. They are the reason why I trust humanity. If it weren't for them, I probably would never come out of my home if I could help it.

Can't stop. Keep going. Save them.

Somehow, I stagger to my feet and hobble forward, a few tiny steps at a time. The agony is seated deep within me, as if my very blood carries pain to every part of my body. It feels like I'm about to be cut in half, and yet I'm nearly there. A few meters more and I'll be within reach of their door. It's open, light spilling out onto the three steps leading up to the porch. A few meters more and maybe I can warn them to watch out. To fight off whatever is coming...

The flash of movement to my left is too fast for any eyes to register properly, even mine. I catch only a flicker of shadow-light-shadow before I'm being lifted into a firm embrace and carried away from the scene. Musk and spice rise around me.

Luc?

I furrow my brow. *Did he do this to my friends?* He didn't seem like the type. He even mentioned how he wanted to help, that he was here in the first place because he had been trying to save a child attacked by two preternatural creatures.

Yet, I can't help but remind myself that he's a vampire. Manipulation is his forte. *Did I save a murderer last night, and in the saving, ensure the deaths of Darrie and Gwen?*

Anger flares within me. I curl my fingers into fists as I continue to wail. Is this somehow my doing? Is Luc planning to kill every living creature he encounters?

Am I about to die, too?

My scream of despair mixes in with the wailing and yet all that emerges is another strangled whisper. "Why, why? Take me back. I need to go back, to warn them..."

"Too late, little banshee." The voice is soft and low and too familiar. I suppress a shudder as he continues to speak. "And it's far too dangerous for you to be out and about in this obviously helpless state."

The words are full of sorrow. Death, and sorrow, and pain. I can't hold it off one second more. My eyes close and I sink into the loss. I'm never going to come back from the agony of *this*.

My fault. My fault. I'm so sorry.

His strong arms continue to hold me tight. His gentle voice, crooning, hints that everything is going to be all right. But it's not. Not after this.

"Death came."

"Yes." He pauses, and then says, "I'm sorry, banshee."

I manage to look up. I am stunned by his wistful expression. Somehow, he's able to retain a haunting beauty even though his features are tainted with angst. It is strange to hear him apologize. Stranger still, it sounds as though he means it.

I blink. My friends are gone, captured by death. Their sentence is not singular, but for both. I feel it. I feel the hollow emptiness that makes up death. I'm *living* it. And nothing will ever be all right again.

Luc

Death came. Oh yes, it came with a vengeance. Aleah's voice is cracked and bereft. I don't think she even knows where she is at this moment. *How the hell did she get herself across the fields in this state?*

I can't carry her back inside her home without permission, and for a while she's too distraught to provide it. I tell her things, sweet things, assurances that it will be okay eventually, in hopes that it will help settle her. It does not work.

There's a swing seat nestled at the edge of her porch, so eventually, I choose to wait there. I have all the time in the world, literally. I will not push her until she's ready. Almost, I wish for the return of the suspicious, guarded creature I met a few hours previously.

I balance her limp body across my lap and rock her as gently as I can. After what seems like hours, she quietens and the soft keening turns into something more like sobs.

"They've both passed on." Her eventual words are full of sorrow. She sits upright. Her face is blotchy and red from all the crying.

The color reminds me of her blood and how much it sings to me.

I curb my body's natural response. This is not the time.

"I'm not surprised."

Hopefully she didn't get a proper look at the state of those two bodies that littered the graveled yard. Bits of arm, pieces of leg, blobs of flesh scattered everywhere. The fact that the elderly male survived as long as he did was testament to what must have been a true fighting spirit. No chance for the woman. From what I could see, her head was torn off in the initial attack.

This killer clearly did not want to feed. It wanted to *destroy*, and with a viciousness I've rarely witnessed even in my extended lifetime.

I don't understand that. Though I may not agree with non-consensual feedings, at least the motive makes some kind of sense.

But this?

This makes no sense whatsoever. Why destroy the innocent? What will that achieve?

"Will you invite me inside, Aleah?" I need answers. Perhaps having someone to talk to will help me find them.

"You again." She hiccups, but her voice is resigned, not resentful, and I know she's coming back to herself. More than that, there's a chance she may now be open to giving me another chance at earning her trust.

"Me again."

"They died horribly." Her gaze is on the dirt covering her feet.

I want to reach out and touch her, remind her that while her friends are gone, she's still here, rooted to this dwelling. She can't remain in this state of sorrow or it will swallow her up whole.

I don't pretend to be ignorant.

"Yes, they did." I pause. I try to remind myself about sympathy and showing it to others in their time of need. "Did you know them well?"

She nods, and wipes snot from her nose with the back of a hand. A streak of mud is left behind. She's going to need a bath when she gets inside. I don't think she even realizes how dirty she is. She's still in shock. I can't blame her.

"They were good friends of mine." A bitter laugh escapes her throat. "I don't have many. And... they were *kind*. Really nice people. Without them I wouldn't have *this* place. Wouldn't have my home, or my business. Or my beautiful bees..."

Tears well in her eyes again, but this time she holds them in. Her eyes look enormous and haunted.

"I'm sorry for your loss." I have another urge to offer her comfort in a physical way. A simple touch, nothing to do with sex. It's not a familiar feeling, and I roll my shoulders to try and curb the impulse.

"They didn't deserve anything bad to happen to them, but especially not...*that*." She keeps talking, and part of me wonders if she realizes I'm even here. "Who would—"

I know the instant the thought hits by her sudden recoil. She seems strong enough to stand, so I slowly release my hold and allow her to slide down off my lap. It's harder than I expect to let her go. I enjoy the way her body heats mine when I hold her.

Once standing, she takes a giant step back, those luminous eyes narrowing in accusation. "Did you—"

"No. I did not." My tone is sharp. I don't know why I'm so offended by her accusation. It makes sense. I am a likely suspect. I am capable of such carnage. And yet, her words make me bristle. Just because I have the capability does not mean I would choose to act in such a vile manner.

After a moment of uncanny stillness, she nods. I

blink. I wouldn't have guessed she could believe me. But she does. The anger vanishes from my system. Slowly, I get to my feet. Now is not the time to spook her.

"But I know who did."

Her gaze snaps to mine. A curious sparkle lights her eyes. I'm glad to see I have not yet lost her to sorrow. If anything, I sense a burning desire for revenge. "Who?"

"One of the rogues who caught me off-guard last night. The vamp." Anger rises in me again, this time directed at myself. I should have stopped them *both*. I should not have been caught off-guard so easily.

A twitch of muscle beneath one eye is her only response.

I briefly lift my healed arm. "I killed the were who disabled me, but the other one got away. I thought maybe he'd have left the area by now, but he is obviously hanging around for some reason."

"Is that normal?" There is hesitation in her tone, as though she's worried. It's strange to hear. She gives the impression of someone strong and fierce, at least, she has in the little time I've known her. Perhaps she's starting to trust me.

My mouth tightens. "Nothing about this situation is normal," I say. I don't want to upset her more, but it's important that I'm honest. "Rogues go loup. They don't think rationally, and they certainly don't work in partnership with anyone else. Blood lust takes them and they kill and run, kill and run. An endless cycle, without thought or calculation, until someone brings them down. *This...*"

I shake my head and stare out into the night, straining to sense anything that might give me a clue as to what the hell is driving the monsters out there hunting humans with such unusual intent. The only sounds beyond standard night creature rustlings are the faint wail of a siren as emergency services make their way presumably toward the tragedy at the neighboring property, and, overlaying it all, Aleah's raspy breath.

"This is all wrong, isn't it?" she asks. Her hand clutches the side of her throat, as though she has batted away loose strands of hair and forgotten to drop her arm back to her side. She looks so vulnerable, I have this sudden urge to take her in my arms, to fit her head against my chest, to reassure her that everything is going to be all right.

The only thing I can do—the only thing I'm willing to do, because she's owed this much—is to be honest with her about this. I will not condescend and try to whitewash everything that has occurred.

"Yes." My answer is crisp.

"Do you think someone is compelling them to do this? Someone, or something... *unnatural*?" Her eyebrows rise.

I'm not sure why she's asking me these questions when she so recently wanted nothing to do with me.

Perhaps, things have changed. I nearly balk at my own stupid thoughts. For her, everything has changed. Now, I am likely a lesser evil.

"It's a possibility." I shrug, unwilling to drag her into this any more than she already has been. *Something unnatural.* I'm beginning to suspect that is exactly what's happening. Unnatural and definitely evil. The rogue behavior seems intentional. Planned, almost. The opposite of what one would expect from a crazed loup. It's calculated and savage at the same time.

She nods, as if it was something she already guessed, and joins me in looking out at the night. Her arms cross over her chest, and I'm not sure if it's because she's cold or if she's protecting herself from the thought of the monsters out there in the dark.

"Did they suffer a lot?" Her question catches me off-guard.

"Your friends?" *How am I supposed to answer that, other than with truth?* "Yes."

"Right." Her arms tighten across her middle.

"I won't lie to you."

She shrugs. "I don't even understand why I asked. I already knew the answer."

"You felt it?"

"Yeah. That's generally how it...works." Her last word falters and she staggers.

I reach out and grab her elbow to steady her, and this time she doesn't shift away from my touch. She must feel worse than she looks, to accept my support so complacently.

"If you let me help you inside, I'll leave immediately, if that's what you wish," I tell her.

"Hmm." A snort escapes her. "Feels a bit like déjà vu. Why are you back here, Luc? What were you doing...*there*? What's your role in all of this?"

She looks at me with narrowed eyes. Her words have tightened like a finger just before the trigger pull.

"Hunting." My grim tone causes her breath to catch, but I shake my head. "Not humans, Aleah. I've already told you I won't take blood by force. I meant what I said."

She shivers, and I heave a sigh and continue.

"I revisited the clearing where I was ambushed and tracked the vamp from there. The scent led me in a wide meandering circle around your property and all the way back to your friends' farm. Unfortunately, I was too late to save them."

She clenches her jaw so hard it pops.

"As was I." Her voice is faint, and after a minute she leans into me. The way her curves mold against my side stirs something in my loins, but now is not the time to explore anything related to lust.

I tighten my arm around her waist and wait for her decision. Her strong floral scent wafts upward and fills my nostril with a subtle beauty. I want to kiss the crown of her head. But I reject my instinct and continue to hold her. She's allowed me this much, and I do not wish to take it for granted.

"All right." She seems exhausted, as if there's nothing left in the tank. "You may enter, Lukey."

This time the ridiculous nickname doesn't bother me. I can tell it's an attempt at reaching out toward something—anything—light-hearted. A feeble attempt, perhaps, but clearly death takes a heavy toll even on those still living. I don't know exactly what it feels like to be a harbinger of death, but from the state of Aleah, it appears to suck the life out of whoever is charged with that miserable task.

No wonder the other banshee I met was so bitter. To live with that level of anguish on a regular basis would likely be enough to turn anyone into a bundle of negativity. Anyone except Aleah. Despite what she must endure on a regular basis, she still retains that sense of lightness and life. I perceive it within her, strong and sure, as clearly as I do her heartbeat. Life force.

She must be a rare creature indeed, to be able to rise above the suffering and cling to life so determinedly. I smile. Her stubbornness is a pain in the ass but it has obviously kept her alive and connected to life instead of wallowing in death.

Right now, though, her reliance on my strength to get her back into the house is a reversal of the previous evening. A swell of something that I can't quite identify rises deep within. It's more than a physical attraction.

That would be easy to recognize. Perhaps it's as simple as the fact that someone needs me, if only for a few minutes, despite what I am and the danger I pose. *She* needs me. The experience of being needed is new, and more enjoyable than I want it to be.

I clear my throat and slowly lead her inside. I'm afraid she'll realize what she's agreed to and pull away from me, rescinding the invitation yet again. For some reason, the possibility of this concerns me and I do not want it to happen.

I'm used to living—and working—alone. As a vampire whose Mistress is no longer in this world, I have no coven. No family. The House was disbanded when the woman who turned us died, and even though another rose in her place and the flock reformed under a new Master, the nature of our Maker's death meant that I have no chance of ever being accepted back in to the fold.

It was my fault she died.

I've been ex-communicated.

My mind shies away from the dark sadness of those early years of isolation. Instead, I focus on the here and now. I have a job and a purpose, and these days my isolation is by choice, rather than necessity. I find I get much done when I'm alone. I only need to rely on myself. I only need to take care of my own needs, and not those of a flock. Much better this way.

When I say alone, though, I don't mean in a physical sense. There is always someone who wants to be fucked by a vamp. Often many "someones", and on occasion, all at the same time. I continue to stay active in the sexual sense. Being undead has heightened those urges and I cannot quell them, even if there are moments when I want to. I enjoy carnal pleasure.

But emotionally? No. Emotion slows you down. Emotion can get you killed. Emotion damn well *hurts*. I avoid it as much as I can.

In my previous—human—life, I knew what it was to love. I knew what it was to be betrayed by that love. Since my turning and ex-communication, I have not needed anyone in that way. Life is easier not needing anyone. I pride myself on the physical connections I make and how separate I keep them from my life.

Until now. No one has stirred any *emotions* in me until the moment a strange pang strikes hard in my chest when I assist a dirt-and-snot-covered little banshee into her home.

"Where's your bedroom?" I ask. I wonder if she'll tell me, especially after what happened the last time I was here.

"Upstairs. But you don't have to—"

"More stairs! Up we go, then." I sweep her back into my arms and she releases a tiny, protesting moan, followed by a long, capitulating sigh. The lack of protest is clear evidence of her current level of exhaustion. Her head flops down to rest on my chest and once again, a strange warmth rises within me.

I swallow. I don't want to think about that right

now. The floral scent tainted with just a bit of honey makes me want to taste her, to kiss her just behind her ear. I shouldn't be this close to her. It's doing strange things to me.

"You're like a bad smell, Lukey," she says, interrupting my thoughts. "Can't get rid of you."

"Charming." My lips quirk up.

Her eyes close and her head lolls. She's gone, wherever banshees go to recharge their inner batteries when the agony of the death call has come and gone.

I sigh and continue up the stairs. It looks like I'll have to figure this out on my own, then.

The fact that she lasted this long before losing consciousness is testament to her inner strength. Aleah's dichotomous mix of fortitude and fragility fascinates me on so many levels, and yet we've hardly had time to get to know one another at all. I want to know her better. And that thought frightens me. I shouldn't want to peel away her layers so I can see what's underneath.

Perhaps you should leave while you're still able.

I glance through doorways as I make my way along the upstairs hallway. A white-tiled bathroom is on the left, almost directly opposite what appears to be a spare bedroom, before we reach the room at the end.

The size denotes this as the main bedroom even before Aleah's scent hits my nostrils. This is definitely where she sleeps. The honeyed notes are every bit as flowery and sweet as the woman herself, and as I rest her now-sleeping form on the bed, I hope she doesn't mind about the mud on that previously pristine white comforter. Too late if she does. *Probably should have removed her boots first.* And maybe wiped her face and hands.

My hands linger on her body longer than they should. I like her warmth.

I glance around to see if I can glean more about this strange, intriguing woman. She seems more human than fae in terms of her general demeanor, but I suspect that's a deliberate attempt to ignore the faerie half of her blood.

Pastel wallpaper, adorned with silvery stripes at various intervals, and delicate white furniture fill the room. Touches of yellow and blue add a restful air. The bed dominates, king-sized and covered with a puffy comforter. I feel suddenly too large, too gauche, and too masculine for this place.

Dare I stay, even for a little while? Will her blood song be too strong to resist? It can't hurt, surely, for at least a few minutes, to keep her company and ensure her recovery is well underway. She's so frail-looking, lying there in the center of that enormous mattress. Surely it would be wrong to leave her alone at this point?

What has gotten into me? I can't remember the last time I cared this much about the emotional welfare of a living, breathing creature. Perhaps I shouldn't have offered to help her. Perhaps I should have simply kept my mouth shut.

I head back up the hallway to locate a wash cloth in the bathroom and return to clean her face and hands. I then proceed to remove her dirt-clad clothing. She's not wearing a bra beneath her top and, finally, when she's laid out on the bed with nothing but a pair of bright pink panties covering her mound, it takes all my strength not to lean in and suck those rose-peaked nipples deep into my mouth.

I let my eyes linger. I give myself time to take in the sight, knowing there's a good chance I won't see it again. I want to memorize the perfection.

My fangs unsheathe at the beauty of her body spread-eagled before me, and my loins tighten at the thought of lapping at her hybrid flesh and sucking on those enticing peaks. Her skin color is creamy rather than white, lush and warm when I run my fingertips experimentally across her belly before reluctantly shifting her onto her side. I need to extract the coverlet from beneath her so I can conceal her sleeping form before my libido takes over and reduces my brain to a state where logic no longer exists.

This is not exactly what I had in mind when I told her I would help. I know that I'm not doing myself any favors by taking advantage of her incapacitated state. Logic and reason war with desire and it's hard to fight at all. I am completely powerless before her and she does not even realize it.

She releases a tiny moan when I roll her, trying to get enough of the quilt out from beneath her that I can cover her properly. That sound is almost my undoing. This woman exudes sensuality and yet, she doesn't even seem to know it. I want to make her moan again. I want the sound to be louder. I want to sink my fangs into her flesh and finally—*finally*—taste the blood that sings so sweetly to my own. I want to mark her. I want others to know she's mine and mine alone.

I clear my throat, which has thickened in tandem with my cock. *Remember, she's off-limits until she wakes.* Instead of doing what I know is the sensible thing and leaving her alone to sleep off the shock, I remove my own boots and clothing, and climb in beside her beneath the covers. It's so natural that it does not even come into question that what I'm doing is completely insane. She will not like this when she wakes up—if she finds me. It's as if I've permanently switched to auto-pilot and am unable to control my actions.

She rolls into my arms, her long body folding itself against mine as easily as if we were made for each other. Two pieces of a puzzle, fitting together perfectly.

Bad idea, man. Bad idea. I keep replaying the cautionary mantra in my head, but it appears my brain is no longer listening.

I shift her dark hair that has fallen in a tangle across her face, and slide one of my arms beneath her shoulder, and then realize my error as she sighs and settles more comfortably into my embrace. If I try to leave now, she'll wake, and I have the feeling she needs plenty of sleep to recover from whatever trauma her banshee soul has just endured.

I have ensnared myself in a spider's web. I have no doubt she will devour me when she wakes, and not in the way I wish. She will be upset at my violation, betrayed by someone she thought she could trust.

I look down at her. There's no tension in her face now. She's calm, vulnerable. She looks younger.

Who is she, this unusual hybrid, and how did she come to be living all the way out here in the wilderness, alone in the middle of mostly empty fields and wooded forest? What is her story? What is her background? And why does she so clearly distrust all vampires?

A vampire ruined my life. Her mention of that fact last night caused an uneasy sensation to settle in my gut. My kind can be vicious. We are, at our core, essentially cruel and predatory, and the thought of Aleah being on the receiving end of a vampire's cruelty fills me with disquiet.

There is a reason I am so fierce in my hunting. There is a reason I have taken it personally to track the perpetrators to this farmland, trying to save these innocent humans. I know what my kind can do. I want to prevent rogues from assaulting the innocent. I do not want all supernaturals blamed for the actions of rogues—in this case, one rogue who seems to be slaughtering purely for sport.

Since the supernatural creatures came out of hiding thirty or so years ago, the world as everyone knew it turned on its axis and eventually resettled into a new normal. It took time, though. Time for those who clung to the old ways to adjust, and realize that the Accord was created for the betterment of all of us, no matter which species or realm we belong to.

Even now, tension still remains in some pockets across the country on both sides. There are some supes who did not wish to announce their existence while there are humans who still do not trust those of us with superhuman abilities to keep our powers controlled. Attacks like those recent ones here only make it more difficult for trust, on either side.

Today, supes mingle alongside humans; fae pass freely between realms as more safe passages open up, and even the existence of angels and demons has been acknowledged as inroads continue to be made into negotiating a peaceful existence for all. Overall, there've been some positive developments to help reduce the fear and anxiety experienced by all sides in relation to living with those different from their own kind.

She's half-fae herself, so Aleah must have always been well aware that there are many things other than human out there, even if her human relatives were the ones to raise her. And there are many things other than *vampire* that cause death and destruction in their wake. It's important that she knows this. I may be a monster, but I am also a lesser evil compared to many others.

Why is she so afraid of *my* kind? What, specifically, happened to make her so close-minded? What did a vampire *do* to ruin her life?

She arches her neck, angling her chin away from me. The movement is clearly unconscious as she sleeps. I catch a glimpse of the regular thump of her carotid, steady and sure. The solid beat fascinates me. I cannot look away.

Without volition, my fangs release from their sheath once again and I bend toward that heady pulse with a low purr emanating from my throat. All questions of her past vanish from my mind. I am solely focused on her throat and how soft the skin will be once I slide my fangs into her.

No. I can't. Not without her permission. Definitely not while she sleeps. Then I will be nothing more than the monster she already assumes I am.

And yet, I can't stop staring at her throat. I watch as the pulse consistently jumps against the flesh, hypnotizing me with its vitality.

I'm more than old enough to feed without draining her, if I wish. She would not feel a thing other than the briefest of pricks and then a slow, sensual whoosh as her blood released into my system. The heady desire that naturally accompanies a feed would ignite her sex and, should I choose, I could lead her to orgasm with a single touch of my incisors. She would see that vampires can deliver pleasure, that we might be monsters but the sensations we provide are not to be found anywhere else.

The lure is almost too much. My fang tips graze her skin and I inhale. *Divine. What an aphrodisiac she would be.*

Her mere scent causes a stirring in my loins. I feel like a young man once again, when sex was new and everywhere and even the caress of silk on my skin was enough to imagine the touch of a lover. I have not felt this way in so long.

I could drink my fill and lick her clean afterward, closing the wound and at the same time sending her into raptures of delight when the orgasm rips through her body. She may feel light-headed from the effects of my bite, though that would be the only downside, unless I chose to drain her fully.

You promised. The whisper through my mind sounds like Aleah's own voice. Low and husky, hardly there at all, and yet all-encompassing in my head as if she has actually invaded my soul.

I hear you, Aleah. I hear you. My growl erupts from the deepest reaches of my chest. *Fuck.* I *did* promise to behave. I don't know why this promise suddenly means everything to me, why it's so important I follow through.

I clench my teeth together, careful to ensure my fangs don't nick my own skin. It's unbearably difficult to turn away from that slow, steady beat, but finally I manage it, only to encounter two sets of accusatory eyes as a pair of Siamese cats watch warily from their perch on the dresser across the room.

"I won't," I insist. "I promised her."

One of the cats continues to stare unblinkingly, but the other narrows it's eyes as if judging me and finding my response wanting.

I don't hate cats, nor do vampires feed on any blood other than human, but right now, with the strength it has taken to turn away from the enticing delight in front of me, I might just transfer my anger elsewhere if they don't hurry from my reach.

Why am I even talking to them in the first place? It's not as though they'll respond, even if they seem to watch me acutely, accounting for every breath I take. I wouldn't be surprised if they leapt from where they sat and started to claw at me if I did something they didn't approve of.

"Go. *Get.*" I release a long low hiss and both arch their backs and race each other to the exit. At the door they turn as if one and hiss right back at me before disappearing down the hallway. I have to admit, their combined hiss is slightly more impressive than my own.

Another whimper comes from Aleah's pouted lips, and my attention returns to my bed partner.

The soft curve of her hip is the perfect resting place for my heat-filled cock. At least, it would be if I knew we were soon to sate its hunger. My God, I want this woman badly, and in so many different ways. And yet it seems as if we're fated to remain unconnected in every respect, unless I break my word and seduce her with a vampire blood call. A call we would both be physically unable to resist.

Could I? The urge grows, becoming almost unbearable.

If I act on this physical need, will she ever forgive me?

Chapter Four

ALEAH

I release a moan as I stretch my arms and legs, arching my back and enjoying the gentle popping sound of stubborn joints loosening up. The stiffness is an unfortunate downside of my human half and the inevitable physicality of working a country property alone. I open my eyes and encounter a pair of icy blues staring down at me.

"What the—"

Luc. I try to roll sideways but his arms are wrapped around me and our limbs are somehow all tangled up together. In my bed? Yep. This is definitely my bed. Skin against naked skin.

Naked? What the actual fuck?

I don't remember how this happened. I would never choose to be almost naked in my bed with an equally almost-naked vampire. I search my memory for answers. Did he break his promise and use his manipulation skills to play tricks on my mind? Did I consent to something I didn't want to do? Then the memories begin to return and I stifle an involuntary sob. *Darrie. Gwen. I'm so sorry. I'm sorry I didn't reach you in time.*

His arms tighten as if sensing my rush of anguish, and then he releases me and sits up. His skin is pale and smooth, the muscles of his torso and shoulders clearly defined and far sexier than I expect. His chest is hairless and I'm not sure why that surprises me. Perhaps the thickness of the tousled mess atop his head caused me to make assumptions about the rest of his body. The faintest line of dark decorates his abdomen, spearing downward to point south somewhere beneath the coverlet. *Point south.* My cheeks heat and I briefly look away to try and regain equilibrium.

He shifts the pillow to a more comfortable position and leans back with his arms folded behind his head, looking all the world as if he truly belongs in that spot.

I shuffle sideways to put some distance between us. "What time is it?"

"It's late. You slept through the night and most of the day. I watched over you while you were out cold. Most of the time, anyway."

Well, that's not creepy at all. "Um, thanks?"

"Except when I slept, too, of course."

"So, you slept here, with me? In my bed?"

"Comfortable mattress." His grin is smug, and for

an instant he looks young and carefree, like a man without a worry in the world. I almost forget he's not human. The urge to lean over and mess up his tousled hair even more almost overtakes me, until all the memories from the previous night suddenly come rushing back in to overwhelm me. *Rogues. Loups. Death.*

I wrap my arms around my middle. "Do you know what happened to my friends?" I decide to sidestep the fact that he's in my bed sans most of his clothing—at least from what I can see. "I need you to explain it to me. Exactly."

His face changes from carefree to somber. "Yes, of course," he says with a nod. I'm relieved that he seems to take the attack seriously. "I slipped back out near dawn to check on the situation. I had just called in the attack to the local authorities when you stumbled into their yard, so I had to choose between sticking around to secure the scene, following the scent of the loup, or ensuring your safety."

He should have followed the loup. He knows it, too. His smug grin has disappeared and the scowl that replaces it transforms him straight back into predatory hunter. It's clear he's upset with himself and his decision. Still, there's a little part of me that enjoys the fact he chose me ahead of duty.

I tamp down that feeling. I don't care one way or the other. Let him choose whatever he wants; it doesn't affect me either way.

At least, it shouldn't.

"The emergency services are likely still on scene. It...will be a lengthy clean-up, I'm afraid."

I try to hide my shudder but I can't. Luc reaches out to touch me and for some reason I don't shift away.

"It was definitely the same vamp I've been tracking. I recognized the scent." He traces a finger around my jawline. His touch is light and strangely welcome. "I'm sorry, Aleah. He got the human female—"

"*Gwen*. Her name was Gwen." I shouldn't be offended by how he referred to her. He doesn't even know her. But I can't help the bitterness that taints my tone. "And her husband was Darrie. They were real people, with names...lives..."

"Yes." Luc's voice softens. "I know."

He pauses, waiting for me to say something, maybe even to keep talking. I appreciate it, but I'm not sure I even know what to say at this point.

Eventually, he starts speaking again. "He got Gwen first, I think. She was farthest away from the house. Looks like she ventured outside, perhaps to check on a noise? The male—Darrie—was found nearer the back door. There was a loaded shotgun beside his body. Silver bullets, too. Unfortunately, he must have been felled pretty quickly as the shotgun hadn't been fired."

"He may have been felled quickly, but his death wasn't fast, though, was it?" I clench my teeth, my fingers balling into tight fists.

"I think..." He hesitates, and then adds, "No. I don't believe it was a quick or easy death for him. Unlike

Gwen's, which I think may have been close to instantaneous. Darrie may have been disabled relatively quickly, but the rest of what happened wasn't either of those things."

"No." I *felt* death coming, and I felt it take them and eventually leave. It took a while, particularly for one of them—Darrie as I know now—and it was agonizing. My only small comfort is that the couple are now together in death as they once were in life. "So, you went back there while I was asleep, and then returned *here* instead of continuing your... tracking? Hunting? Whatever you call it."

"Hunting. And yes, it's part of my job, to liaise with the local cops. Your town policeman—Bernie—seems to be pretty clued up about the situation already. Apparently, there have been a few cases of livestock being taken in the past weeks, and he'd already been liaising with my unit about the vicious nature of those attacks. Add to that the young boy who was taken a couple of nights ago..."

A young boy? I blink, and pull back to look at him carefully. That must have been the death I experienced the other night. A remembered pang sets my heart thumping painfully as Luc continues talking.

"It's the reason the department sent me here in the first place."

"And returning *here*...to my *bed*?" Now that I understand what happened to my friends, I need to understand what is happening with me...and him.

"Well, you know. I just wanted to...check on you again."

If I didn't know for sure that vamps can't blush, I'd think he had a touch of pink in those angular cheeks. It's actually endearing, a word I never thought I could associate with a vamp.

"And then it was morning," he continues. "I couldn't venture out in the daylight, of course."

"Of course." I don't hide the dryness that taints my tone. "And how did undressing me—*and* yourself— right down to our underwear factor in to that?" My cheeks start to heat up even though I'm the one asking the questions. *At least he left my knickers on.* I don't wear a bra so I can't exactly blame him for that one.

"You were covered in dirt and mud, and you were freezing to the touch." Though he speaks faster than usual, everything about him is casual, as though this is nothing to be upset about. "I wanted to put you beneath the comforter, and it seemed like the right thing to do, to get your clothing off first."

I raise a brow. "Mm hmm."

"And of course, I couldn't leave you without helping you warm up, and the best way to do that was... with *this*." His tone is conceited as he waves a hand, indicating himself, before swinging his legs to the side to perch on the edge of the bed. I almost snort, but manage to hold myself back.

"There's no way a snuggle under the covers with a

vamp would make any difference to my core body temp—yikes!"

He didn't bother to leave his own knickers on. He conveniently ignores my comment—and my no doubt goggle-eyed stare—as he calmly moves around the room collecting his clothing. I try to look anywhere but at his manly package, though I can't help but sneak a glance or two his way. He seems to display no hint of embarrassment whatsoever and honestly, if I had a body as perfectly proportioned as his, I might not be embarrassed to show it off, either.

Surreptitiously, I slide the comforter right up to just beneath my chin.

I'm not quite sure how to react. Part of me wishes I had access to my stake so I could pierce his heart for entering my bed without any clothes on. The other part of me, the part that should be way more ashamed of herself, allows me to stare a little too long.

Who knew a naked vampire body could be quite so alluring? Who knew a vampire's rear end would be shapelier than any I've ever seen in my life? Who knew I would be tempted to touch him, to see if it is as firm as it looks? Not that I've seen many naked rear ends. Not that I've felt any. His arse is tight and firm and my mind fills with images of that tight ass squeezing and pumping hard as he thrusts into someone in a frenzied and sensual coupling.

He turns at that moment and my breath hitches in

my throat. *Holy moly*! Who knew Luc was hiding *that* much tackle in his trousers?

Let's not mention how enticing his rippling muscles and smooth skin looks as he reaches for his discarded shirt and pulls it back on over his head. Let's *definitely* not mention the warmth that rushes through me, pooling between my legs and making a mockery of my previous comment. Clearly there's more than one way for a vampire to impart warmth to another being.

I swallow, sitting up and adjusting the bed cover to ensure I continue to retain at least a small degree of modesty.

Luc's grin widens. It's like he can read my mind. The bastard does enjoy stirring the pot, that's for sure.

"I like your choice of underwear, Aleah. Pink was not what I expected. You seem more like the black and brooding sort."

"*God damn it!*" This whole situation is beyond uncomfortable. At least—as far as I can tell—he didn't sneak any of my blood. I decide the best path is to pretend to ignore the no-clothes issue for the moment. I tighten my grip on my sheets, forcing myself to continue. "Tell me more about these rogues. Have you been tracking them for a while? Are you an official hunter? You've mentioned your department a few times. I assume...an investigative one?"

He nods. "I have been tracking both the vamp, and his rogue partner, for several months. They were in Melbourne, causing havoc out in some of the more affluent suburbs. We lost track several weeks ago until we got the call about unusual livestock butchery near Hatton Grove. I suppose I am an official hunter, though we call ourselves vampire police these days." While he talks, he pulls on a pair of jeans and bends to lace his boots. When he straightens, he raises a hand and runs long fingers through already messy hair. It gives him a rakish look that adds to the sexiness. I decide to ignore that too, though the squiggle of desire that feels a little bit like butterflies in the belly once again makes a liar of my intentions.

"Vampire police." I arch a brow. "That's a real thing?"

"Oh, yes, we're real. I work for SUDAP—otherwise known as the Supernatural Division of the Australian Federal Police."

I try to stay away from the mainstream, out here on the farm, and don't really keep up with the news or general politics. But even I've heard of SUDAP. It stands to reason they would be just as likely to employ supernaturals as humans—probably more so, I guess —but I hadn't really thought about that before now. And if he's employed by SUDAP, Luc really must be one of the good ones. Their vetting process is supposedly more rigorous than that required for the standard police. Which means it's a good idea that I trusted him.

"So, you're a vampire detective."

"Sergeant," he corrects. It's clear his title is significant but he takes no offense.

"Sergeant Durand," I say. His lips quirk briefly as I try out the name. It suits him. "How did you come to be in a job like that, Luc? And for that matter, how old are you?"

I want to get dressed but I know he won't give me privacy. Plus, I'm interested in the conversation we're having. I don't want it to stop. He's being forthcoming with me, which I appreciate.

"How old are you?" he shoots back.

"Twenty-nine." It's an easy number for me to admit. I have no shame in my age. I've learned that being haunted by death makes me appreciate all the ways in which I'm reminded I'm alive.

"Ah." He smiles gently, and I sense rather than see the implicit weariness behind the smile. "You've never known anything other than the Accord years."

I shrug. He's right. I was born a year after the Accord came into being, though fat lot of good it did for my poor father. I don't tell him this, though. It's not something he needs to know. At least not right now.

"I've been on the Force since they opened it up to my kind twenty-seven years ago. You would have been two."

"Well, I'm all grown up now." I have no idea why that pops out. I duck my head to avoid the humor in his stare and wish away the heat prickling my cheeks.

"So you are." His voice hums with awareness, forcing my gaze back to his. I can't tell if he's agreeing with my statement or if there's more behind his words. A dirty insinuation, perhaps? It doesn't come across sleazy, however. "But I'm still a damn sight older than you."

At my raised brow and silence, he capitulates.

"Two hundred and eighty-six. I was turned the night of my thirty-sixth birthday."

My brows raise. "Whoa. That must have sucked."

He snorts gently. "Yes, it did. Literally and figuratively." Then he shrugs. "It gets easier the longer it goes on. I can hardly remember my human life anymore."

He says it nonchalantly, but I pick up an undertone of sadness. I imagine it is easier as the remembrance of being human fades, but it must be sad to lose a part of you, even if it's just memories. Does that mean he's a different person now than he was as a human?

I know vamps can live hundreds, even thousands of years, and their power grows with time. Technically, like hybrid fae, they're close to immortal, but their violent nature often means they don't live out their potential. At more than two hundred and eighty years of age, that most likely makes Luc one of the more powerful of his kind.

A shiver runs through me, even though I'm certain by now that Luc has no intention of hurting me. It's not a shiver born of fear.

His sharp gaze catches my tremble even though the

comforter still surrounds me. His mouth twists. "You're safe, little banshee. I fed again last night, before I returned here."

He busies himself rummaging through my chest of drawers and I'm so distracted by what he has just admitted that I don't bother trying to stop him, even though he has probably just seen my extra stash of wooden stakes and the silver knife I keep buried in my top drawer.

He fed last night? "So, you went off and...had sex with someone? And then..." *Returned to my bed?* "Where?"

He stills for a moment, looking down into my drawer rather than back at me. The stillness exudes annoyance even though I can't see his face. "Sex and feeding often go hand-in-hand, Aleah, though not always. And last night was pure sustenance. I *fed* only. No sexual pleasure involved, sadly."

Not that it's any of my business. At least, it shouldn't be.

"Oh." I wish I could sink right down under this coverlet to hide the acuteness of my embarrassment. *I don't care.* I'm not supposed to care. Really.

And yet, I do.

"As to where I feed?" He picks out a random top and a pair of sweatpants. "Back in Melbourne, it's mostly at bars and clubs, where the prey is willing and able. *Very* willing and able, believe me."

He tosses the clothing my way. I quickly shuck on

the top, grateful for the protection it affords.

"Out here in the sticks it's usually the local hotel. Do you know The Royal?"

I pull the pants underneath the comforter and wiggle them on as best as I can while ensuring the comforter stays securely over me.

"Yes," I say, once I'm dressed. I still keep the comforter around me only because there's a chill in my room and I don't need him looking at my nipples the whole conversation. Not that he would. But I don't want to give him an excuse. "I have dinner there sometimes, after I've been into town to drop off my wares at the local craft shop."

Who from Hatton Grove would voluntarily go with a vamp? Someone I know? Has an altogether different kind of feeding been taking place, while I've been obliviously eating in the downstairs restaurant in the Royal Hotel?

"I have a room there for the duration of this investigation."

These are people I might know.

His grin has no humor in it whatsoever. In this moment he looks exactly like what he is—a predator. "Perfect for someone like me."

"Do you ever...?" I can't bring myself to finish the question.

He guesses my intent, his eyes flaring with irritation beneath furrowed brows.

"Despite what you might think, I don't kill innocents, Aleah." He closes my dresser drawer, his back to me. I try not to drop my eyes and check out his ass again. "I feed on *willing* participants, and I only take what I need to survive. I *never* take more than they're able to give, and they always walk away satisfied afterward."

Satisfied? In what way? I might not be able to admit to him that the reason for the sick feeling in the pit of my stomach stems from jealousy, but the least I can do is admit that truth to myself.

Until yesterday, I would never in a million years have considered taking a vampire lover, but since Luc stumbled into my life, I can't seem able to *stop* thinking about it. What would it be like to receive pleasure from someone fully capable of killing me? Does that make me twisted?

After a moment of awkward silence, I nod. "I believe you."

"Hmm. How generous." His accompanying snort speaks volumes, and the urge to grin rises up. It shocks me. I never feel anything close to enjoyment for days following a death call, and for just a few seconds, Luc's snippiness almost tips me over into laughter.

My burgeoning smile dies as the horror of what happened seeps back in to my thoughts. The shift in mood must show in my features, because Luc is around the bed in a flash. He wraps one arm across my shoulders and squeezes tight.

"I'll find him, banshee," he says. It's strange that he's offering me comfort when he doesn't seem to be the type. It's stiff, but the effort is there. And I appreciate that. "I promise you. And when I do…"

My heart thumps painfully.

"When you do, I hope you *kill* him. *Slowly.*"

I can't believe I just uttered those words. Death is the worst thing I can think of and the one thing I would normally not wish even on my worst enemy. In this case, though, I can't think of anything I want more than the slow and painful demise of the one who put my friends through such agony.

His grip tightens and his voice is fierce when he answers. "Oh, I will, believe me. I will."

I'm slightly surprised to find his determination as strong as mine. I wonder why. I'd always imagined there was some kind of loyalty among supernaturals. Then again, technically, I'm a preternatural creature too, and I feel no loyalty toward those who would harm the innocent.

I rest my head against his shoulder.

"Be careful," I say. I'm not sure why I tell him this. Surely, he knows how to take care of himself? "Your injuries the other night were pretty severe."

"Thank you." He pauses and shifts uncomfortably, as though he, too, wasn't expecting my care. "I appreciate your concern. I know now how fast and strong these rogues are. Even though only one remains —as far as we know—they both displayed more strength than any supe I've ever seen, loup or not. It was as if they were being…"

"As if...*what*?" I scrunch my nose and tilt my head so I can look at him more easily.

"Never mind." He shakes his head, staring straight ahead at my wall. He seems to be deep in thought. "Put some pants on, Aleah. Your scent is far too enticing."

Now that sounds like a diversion to me. I keep my head upright so I can glare at him with narrowed eyes, but he just stares back unblinking, with the fake light of innocence giving a hint of green to the usual blue. For the briefest of moments, I forget why I'm staring at him. He's beautiful.

"My pants *are* on," I remind him, after an awkward pause.

He gives me a grin and shrugs. "Then your scent is far too alluring no matter what," he says. "You continue to be a distraction."

I decide it's best not to say anything in return. He's still prevaricating. Darrie and Gwen were *my* friends, and if Luc won't tell me all he knows, I'll just have to find out for myself another way.

Something evil is going on in the Hatton Grove region, and I'm not four years old anymore. This time, I won't sit back and watch while wicked things continue to happen to the few people in this world I care about. This time, I'm going to sound a warning cry time, and even though my voice is defective as fuck, I'm going to make damn sure everyone who needs to hear my warning, does so in time to save a life.

The only question is, how?

LUC

Aleah finally climbs out of bed and pulls on a fresh pair of socks and shoes. Something has shifted in her these past few minutes. I can't quite put my finger on it, but she has a gleam in her eyes that wasn't there earlier, and a determined set to her shoulders that concerns me.

"Don't do anything stupid, little banshee," I say, as she laces up the white sports trainers.

"I don't know what you mean." When she speaks, she doesn't look at me. Instead, she keeps her focus on her task, hair falling down to cover her face. "Of course, I won't."

She stands and meets my gaze with a clear expression and a faint smile that I don't trust one little bit.

"I mean it, Aleah." I understand that people dear to her heart were killed last night, but that doesn't mean she should do anything reckless in order to exact revenge. "The rogue, or potentially rogues, are not operating under any set of rules I've ever observed. I can't protect you if you go off half-cocked."

Her soft laughter fills the room and my heart squeezes painfully at the sound. I may not have a heartbeat, but my body knows the sound of perfection when it arrives. *She should laugh all the time.*

I *want to make her laugh.*

"First off, I have no cock," she says. "Being half-cocked would be *your* area of expertise, I believe, and I'm very sorry for you if that is the case."

I open my mouth and snap it shut again. I'm not sure what to say to that. It's as though she's trying to be humorous but she's also determined to do whatever she has set in her pretty little head. I'm not sure whether to laugh or be cautious.

"Second," she continues, raising her fingers and ticking her reasons off. "You arrived in my world exactly two nights ago. I've been managing perfectly fine on my own for many years now, and I don't need you to start 'protecting' me. In fact, I seem to recall that if it wasn't for my intervention, you'd be a little pile of dust and ashes right about now."

She raises her brows, daring me to contradict her. She's looking for a fight, I realize. She wants to let her aggression out. What can I say? She's correct, except for one thing.

"I'm *never* half-cocked," I say firmly.

Her glance down at my groin is brief but it's enough. My organ wants to reach permanently skyward whenever I'm anywhere near this woman, and one look from her sends the damn thing soaring once again. Perhaps she can be persuaded to fight me in this way, with our bodies battling for dominance. The flesh strains against my zippered jeans and for once I welcome the rush of desire, encouraging my cock to full expansion rather than trying to tamp it down. My fangs follow suit and I grin, ensuring the now-unsheathed incisors are clearly visible.

Her breath catches and pink stains her cheeks. I step forward and put one finger firmly under her chin until she has no choice but to tilt her face up to meet mine.

"Half-cocked is not in my vocabulary."

She swallows. I watch her throat bob and my groin twitches involuntarily. I lean in, intending to take her mouth in a punishing kiss, but change tack at the last moment and nip lightly at her full bottom lip with my teeth. One of my fangs accidentally nicks her plump flesh. Blood seeps out, just enough for me to taste her. My eyes roll back. I nearly collapse. Need flashes through me at the taste and a huge shudder wracks my body. *Jesus, fuck, but she tastes like fucking heaven.*

I want more. I want to drink her dry. I want...

I let out a breath. I need to control myself around her. And she makes it almost impossible.

I lick at a tiny droplet of blood that hovers on her

lip, unable to resist its call. The accompanying wave of desire is so intense a groan ratchets up out of my throat. "Sorry." I start to twist away but her slender hands grip the side of my head and hold me in place. I freeze, slowly opening my eyes. Her gaze is no longer clear and innocent. Instead, I read lust and confusion in equal parts. She craves me, and yet she doesn't understand why.

"I want you to kiss me," she admits. "And yet..." She frowns briefly, jutting out her bottom lip.

"It goes against everything you thought you wanted?" I rip my eyes away from her lip. It's torture to do something so simple.

"Yes." She nods once, not realizing the effect every movement has on me.

"Your blood is like a drug to me, Aleah," I admit. Perhaps I shouldn't. Perhaps I should keep these thoughts to myself due to the fact that she could very well force me out of her home once again. I don't want to scare her into sending me away, and yet, I can't stop talking. There's a fierce need inside of me to be honest. "Even the one droplet I coaxed from your lips a moment ago is enough. It sings to my blood, and when that happens, it will be the same in reverse for you."

I want her to know. I *need* her to know just how pleasurable it will be for her. I want her to want this too. I want her to be open to trying sex with a vampire. With *me*. I want her to let me prove myself worthy of her. She won't regret it.

Her eyelids half close and her mouth parts slightly. "It *is* the same," she says. "That's *exactly* how it feels. As if your body is singing to mine...calling me...*seducing* me...I didn't think I wanted it. And yet, somehow, I can't stay away."

She sounds helpless. I like it. It's wrong; it's twisted in so many ways, but I love her being so vulnerable.

My groan is louder this time. "Why do you think I keep coming back?" I ask. My voice is rough now, low and husky. "I need to taste you, Aleah. I need to see if you're exactly how I envision you. And yet, I'm sure you'll exceed my expectations."

"How can you possibly know that?" Her eyes are hooded but some part of her obviously still clings to her rationality. I want to squander that part of her. I want to make it disappear.

"Because of that tiny drop I've already tasted." I bring my head close to hers, allowing our foreheads to touch. "Let me, Aleah. Let me show you just how good it can be."

I don't pull back. Instead I wait, and hold my breath even though I don't need to breathe at all.

"Okay." One word uttered in that soft breathy voice. One word only, and yet so powerful. One word, and my cock is already at attention, ready to go. *Fuck.*

Her eyes snap up to meet mine. "As long as you stop if I say so."

Oh, Jesus. "I don't know if—"

I don't manage to finish the sentence. This time her

lips take mine, and I'm lost in a haze of delight as our mouths and tongues dance in rhythm. My fangs pierce her flesh once more, this time with permission. The zing of her hybrid blood infuses my veins with life, calling to the vampire within. The taste is everything I dreamed it might be, and a thousand times better.

My growl turns to a purr and the ache in my groin is both agony and ecstasy.

Her answering moan directly into my mouth is more a vibration than a sound. Desire hits new heights —heights I never imagined I would discover, even in a supposedly close-to-immortal lifetime. The fact that this feels just as good for her—even though I knew it would—only adds to my pleasure. For once, it's not just about me. It's about wanting to make her feel as good as I do.

Ripples of sensation traverse my skin, from my scalp right down to my toes.

I break away from her mouth, breathing hard even though I don't have to, but it feels like the only way to let out some of the emotion squeezing at my chest. She makes me feel almost human.

"What are you doing to me, little witch?"

Her fingers trace a line down my throat and pause at the top button of my shirt.

"Call me fae, if you wish," she says. Her voice is husky and it's like she is casting a spell of pleasure. "Or call me human. That's who I am. I'm not a witch."

"Oh, I know that, little banshee-human hybrid." I

grin. "If you were, I'd not be trembling so hard with the effort of holding back my need. Witches don't carry the same allure for a vamp."

Her smile is slow and seductive, and my whole body responds to its attraction.

"Wow, you really *are* trembling, Luc," she says. Her voice drops an octave, and I detect amusement as well as desire. She tilts her head to the side so the column of her throat is exposed and I nearly swear. She must know what she's doing to me. "Is my blood really that potent, or do you just enjoy the thrill of the chase? What will happen if I give in and let you fuck me?"

The words are a douse of cold water on my lust, and yet there's a look in her eye that still hints at the promise of something more. She's giving out mixed messages but... *That look.* It heats my ardor as effectively as a courtesan's practised hand. Is she teasing me? Is she serious? I honestly don't know at this point.

She continues to work at the buttons of my shirt, popping open the first one and continuing lower, one after the next, tracing patterns on my exposed skin as she descends. If I were human, I'd have lost my load already. The wench is clearly experienced at this, despite her previous supposed air of innocence.

My anticipation at what she may do next only grows. However, there's a small part of me that wishes I had been the one to consume her first, that I snagged her innocence and made her mine in every sense of the word.

This time, my growl is lower, erupting from the depths of my belly.

"Human. Fae. Whatever you are, if you don't stop right now"—I grab her hand, clasping her wandering fingers tightly within my grip to hold her in place—"there's no guarantee what might—"

My voice is helpless. Desperate. I'm pleading with her. It's less than becoming but I don't care. I can't. Not when she holds such power.

"Words, vampire." Her eyes are half slits now, the irises almost an iridescent green behind the shield of her lowered lashes. "Are you going to back them up with action?"

Challenge accepted.

I move so fast she has no time to react. Her delicious body mashes against mine with a perfection that seems as if we're physically made for one another.

She has already made quick work of my shirt, so I shuck it off the rest of the way and let it fall to the ground. The shapeless top and sweatpants I grabbed from her drawer are anything but sexy. Nothing alluring that I can unbutton in a slow and sensual return dance. And yet, she still looks more beautiful to me than supermodels in silky lingerie walking down a catwalk. All good. Fast suits my current mood just fine.

I rip the top up over her head and toss it to one side. Those lush breasts present themselves once again to my view, the rose-colored nipples instantly peaking. This time, I'm not letting her go until I taste my fill.

I cradle one of the creamy globes in my palm and lift it slightly, then bend my head to suckle at the enticing tip. Her gasp is soft but the moan that follows is not. "Luc, I don't think this is...oh, *fuck!*"

The curse is released when I bite down, hard. Her blood spills into my mouth. Metallic. Honey-scented. Divine. The delicious aphrodisiac fills my being until I can't see, hear, or feel anything but the delightful liquor flowing into me from her.

Her hand instantly reaches for the back of my head, cradling me there, holding me in place. Her fingers bury themselves in my hair, curling and tugging at the roots.

Lifeblood. Life force. Everything I want. Everything I need. Everything I can never be again.

I suck, and lick, and tug as I feed, as much like a babe at its mother's breast as any helpless newborn. Aleah's blood is my sustenance. *Heaven.* There is nothing left in my mind or my body but the succulent taste of *her.* The scent of her blood, so freely offered, has me completely undone.

After what seems like aeons, I become aware of two things. Her hand on my cock, kneading and exploring, and her gentle sobbing, as if her heart is about to break in half.

It takes massive effort, but I wrench up my head

from her delectable breast, and lick the bite wound to promote fast healing.

I manage to look her in the eye, noting the tears running down her face.

"I made you cry." On some level I know that is significant, but I'm still so lost in the haze of desire that I don't really care at this moment about anything other than taking ownership of this beautiful creature's body.

I kiss her briefly, the taste of her lips once again filling my senses with light and hope and joy. What she gives out is in complete contrast to the tears still falling from her iridescent eyes.

"Why, Allie? Why are you crying? It's not supposed to hurt. Do you not enjoy the sensation of my feeding?"

Am I doing something wrong? Am I hurting her in any way? If it's the case, I will remove myself from her vicinity. And yet, the thought of moving even an inch makes me want to writhe in pain.

Her breathing labors, as if she's run many miles without pause, and I reach up to swipe at one of the tears with my thumb. She jerks away from my touch and, against every instinct, I let her go. It feels as though someone has reached into my chest cavity, wrapped their fingers around my heart, ripped it out of me, and crushed it. The phantom pain nearly causes me to stagger forward and collapse.

She shifts back out of my embrace and reaches for her top, holding it in front of her bare breasts like protection. My manhood throbs, needing her to stay close. This does not bode well for my intention to claim her as mine.

"It didn't hurt," she says, looking down at her hands. "At least, not after the first bite that felt like the lightest pinprick. I enjoyed it. A lot. But I don't *want* to." Her voice is hoarse and she clears her throat as if it's difficult to get out the words.

What has her so conflicted?

"Surely you've been with men before?" I ask, my voice rough and quick. "Desire is as natural as breathing, to a human. More so, for a fae, in my experience. What is your problem? Is it the blood?"

"It's not the blood." Her face turns stony. "It's your *kind*. What you do. Or at least, what you've all done in the past."

My kind. "Police?"

"Don't be obtuse."

I grin, deliberately displaying my unsheathed fangs. "No matter what *kind* I am..." I fling the word back at her, allowing my hurt to show. "I am working now to find and stop a killer, before more innocent people die. I'm sorry you have a problem with me, Aleah. I damn sure regret that we can't enjoy each other's bodies fully before I leave. It would have been...*spectacular* for you."

She rolls her eyes. "Arrogant fuck."

Out of nowhere, she drops the top, stepping forward to clasp my upper arms. *What is she doing?* The tips of her breasts almost, but not quite, touch my chest. I take a deep breath in, forcing my lungs to capacity, and am rewarded when the expansion allows her nipples to graze my skin. The touch ignites heat where skin touches skin. Thank all that's holy that I haven't yet put back on my shirt and stormed out of here in a huff. It just reinforces the fact that my arrogance can be quite charming, whether she wants to admit that or not.

Beyond that one long breath I freeze, not quite sure which way her mood will swing, and not wanting to jinx anything. She taps a thumb against my bicep, as if considering her next move.

"I'm beginning to see that maybe my aunt was wrong in what she taught me," she says slowly. It's almost as if she doesn't quite believe her own words.

Her hands move up over my shoulders to my pecs.

"Hell, maybe *I* was wrong," she continues. She's talking more to herself than to me. As long as she keeps touching me the way she is, I don't care. I'll listen until she stops. "Just because bad stuff happened a long time ago in my life, doesn't mean all vampires are evil."

If I had a beating heart, it would be working frantically right now. My loins have definitely received an up-and-down workout since meeting Aleah.

"No species is all good or all evil, Allie." I can barely force the words out. My mouth has gone dry.

"Not human, not fae, and certainly not vampire. Does this mean—"

She wriggles her pelvis, teasing my flesh back to full erection and making me forget my train of thought.

"Shut up and kiss me again, Luc," she commands. There's a serious glint in her eyes now. "Only this time, don't stop until we reach the *spectacular*."

Chapter Six

ALEAH

I'm pretty sure this is a bad idea. But I don't pull away from Luc.

The instant flare of almost-emerald in his normally blue eyes says everything about want and need. With a low, animal-like growl that ratchets up my own desire ten-fold, his mouth devours mine, and this time, I let him fully in. It's a decision I didn't think I would ever make, but this whole ordeal has surprised me, especially with how easy it has been to give in to Luc. I'll have to dissect that later. But for now, I allow myself to surrender to the need that has been vibrating within me ever since he first landed on my doorstep.

His kisses are like nothing I've ever experienced before. Despite his earlier assertion that I must have been with others, I'm not at all experienced. I've kissed a few men, but he will be my first lover, if I have the courage to let it go that far.

I'm not sure if that's something I want to share with him. At first, I'm hoping he'll be patient, and go slowly, but I don't think he will unless I say something. And I'm afraid if I do, he'll want to stop.

He takes my mouth in a way that both demands and gives, in equal measure. Like he is claiming ownership. And the feeling of being owned, being someone's possession, is something I never thought I would ever enjoy. It has never crossed my mind as something to strive toward, as something to be proud of, but heat flares through my body as quickly as fireworks shoot across the sky. Every nerve, every inch of my flesh, is hypersensitive to the touch of his skin against mine. It's almost painful. I don't want it to stop.

As the kiss progresses, my need grows. Now I want him to take me, hard and fast. It completely contradicts my earlier feelings of preferring slow and steady. As long as he takes me, as long as he makes me see stars and the moon and makes me forget my own name, I don't care how he does it. I *need* him to make me forget everything that has happened in the past few days. Everything, except this delicious ache that continues to grow and center in the plump bud between my legs.

He tastes clean and slightly minty. *Did he use my toothpaste while I slept?* The tip of his tongue flicks in and out, dancing with mine, the connection sending an army of shivers to traverse my body. I can't help the moan that escapes me, but he captures that quickly and moans in return, our shared desire spiraling upward. Still the kiss goes on.

His urgent fingers trace patterns on my back. I arch into the caresses, my hips rocking back and forth of their own accord, using the hardness and heat of his erection to increase my own ardor. Wet slickness coats my seam and I break away from his kiss, panting heavily and trying to understand exactly what is happening to my body.

I want him. So much. I want him inside me. Now.

When his mouth drops to my neck, nuzzling along the path of my carotid artery, I manage to say in a voice made breathless with anticipation, "Take me, Luc. *Please.*"

He chuckles against my neck, the sensation sending tremors of heat in all directions. "Did you say, taste?"

"*Take!*" I can hardly catch my breath at all. My whole body is on fire. "Or taste. Do either. Do both. I don't care. Just do—*Oh!*"

This time when his fangs pierce my skin there's no pain whatsoever, not even the faint sense of a pinprick that I felt earlier when he bit down on my nipple. Instead it's almost a tickle, like the softest caress of breath. I don't quite know what he's doing, or how, but the rush of warmth in my neck spreads throughout my whole body, right out to my fingertips and toes, until it circles back again and centers right where it has the most impact. It's as if he's introduced a sex-seeking drug to my blood and my body cooperates by carrying it super-fast along every vein. The heat reaches into every nook and cranny of my body. Every inch of my being. Coalescing at my core. It makes me want more. I *crave* him. I crave everything about him.

"Oh, my *God!*" This level of sensation is insane. I can't believe I'm doing *this*, of all things. With *Luc*. But I don't care.

I can't hold on. He continues to suckle and whatever he's doing pushes me beyond any place of sensuality I've experienced in the past. The crescendo builds until it bursts through me, unable to be contained a moment longer, and I tip over the edge into a crazy, bucking climax.

My legs collapse beneath me and I let out a muffled shriek as my whole body begins to rock with the force of the orgasm. His strong arms catch me as I buckle. He lifts me with ease, and I wrap my legs around his waist, working more by instinct than anything else, and tilt my pelvis to prolong the exquisite pressure against my pulsing clit. His hands spread-eagle my butt cheeks, fingers reaching in to explore my slit through the thin fabric of my sweats, stilling when he reaches my still-spasming channel entrance.

"Your sweatpants are in the way."

"Rip them off." *What the actual fuck has come over me?* These sweats are my favorite comfy old— "Oh, *my.*"

He rips them apart, right down the center seam.

Well, I can't blame him. He did exactly as I asked. As the two halves of my favorite sweatpants and the underlying pink underwear sag away to the sides, he dips into my slit with a forefinger. One swipe and I'm primed and ready yet again. How is that even possible?

"You're wet. So wet." His voice is thick and I raise my eyes to his. They're ablaze now, like bright emeralds. No blue left at all. I feel as if I could lose myself in their brilliant depths. I force my gaze back down, to his lips, and realize his mouth is coated in blood. *My blood.* A droplet descends from the corner of his lips.

I don't think, just react, leaning in to lick the droplet from his chin. His shocked gasp is reward enough. The taste is metallic and kind of gross.

"Ew." I wrinkle my nose, and he laughs at my distaste. I realize it's the first time I've heard a genuine laugh from him since we met, and the sound makes me long for more. "That is seriously not nice."

His grin widens, the fangs showcased in full force. "Oh, I think we'll have to agree to disagree on that one, Aleah."

In this moment, at least on the surface, he looks exactly like what he is—a predator triumphantly holding aloft his prey. And yet, underlying the predator, I read a faint hesitancy in his manner. He's not one hundred percent sure how I'm going to react. In his uncertainty, I see the man as well as the vampire, and that fact in itself is an aphrodisiac.

"I want you, Aleah." His tone is husky and sends shivers up and down my body. But there's also hesitation. Does he still think I'll reject him? "Will you let me take you?"

My heart pounds and dizziness fills my head. A tiny part of my brain wonders if it's because he took too much blood. Is my heart trying to compensate by speeding up until it almost jumps out of my chest?

Somehow, though, the other part of me knows, without really understanding how, that he wouldn't allow that to happen. He may feed, or taste, or make it part of the mating ritual, but he won't drain me dry, nor let harm come to me in this situation. I don't know *how* I know that for sure, but I do. And that, in turn, reassures me that I want this. I want to feel him inside of me. I want him to take me in a way I haven't been taken before.

"Yes." I nod once. "I want that. But I want it fast."

There's a pause before he says, "I can accommodate that request."

He trails kisses across my jawline.

I tilt my head back, offering him more access to my throat. In one swift movement, he swivels and throws me backward onto the mattress. His actions are such a blur that even my half-fae eyes can't keep up. He undresses and only a nano-second later is lying atop me on the bed. His desire presses against my thigh.

"As a vamp I have no illness to pass on, nor active seed with which to make a child," he assures me. "You will not need protection, little banshee, nor will you want it."

My heart lurches again. I hadn't even thought of that. Many years ago, when I was still living with my aunt in the city, the other girls at school all got their periods and I did not.

"You're a half-breed," my aunt explained. "Half-breeds are neither one thing, nor another. You won't ever get your period like the human girls, but you'll also never be able to bear a child of your own, like a full fae."

I wasn't sure how I felt about that information at the time, only because having kids wasn't something that had ever crossed my mind. I was grateful that I didn't have to worry about a period, however. I saw girls struggle with it every month, and in order to keep up appearances, I faked having one too. But I didn't know what it was like, not really.

I'd completely forgotten that conversation until this moment. With Luc poised above me ready to enter, the memory returns, as does the faint sense of sadness at never being able to reproduce.

There's something else I should have told him before this moment. "I—"

Too late. The head of his organ finds my channel entrance and he thrusts hard and fast, just like I asked of him. I do not think he even heard me try to tell him. The pain leaches through my body in an unexpected wave. At my muffled shriek he stills instantly.

There's a heavy silence between us. I can feel him shift slightly, careful, as if afraid he's going to hurt me. His gaze is burning and bright as his eyes scan my face.

"What the...you're...a *virgin*?" he finally asks.

I continue to hold onto his shoulders, though my grip has lessened considerably as my body adjusts to his size. I look away, unable to keep his gaze. "Um, yeah."

"Why didn't—"

"Probably should have mentioned it, huh?"

"Yes." His teeth are gritted, the fangs hanging down over his bottom lip, and the rictus of concentration on his face is testament to the control it must be taking him to remain still. "Probably should have."

I clear my throat. "Well, now that you're *in*, so to speak..."

"I am definitely *in*."

The initial pain has receded, and I wiggle my hips experimentally. He groans above me, the sound heartfelt. "Don't do that, little one, unless you want to finish this fully."

"What makes you think I don't want to finish this?"

If I was capable of rolling my eyes in this moment, I would. How much more obvious does a girl need to be? Now that the pain has ebbed, the sensation of fullness rises. *He's so big.* How is it possible for my body to house all of those magnificent inches? The pressure in what feels like every part of my belly increases the pleasurable ache between my legs. *I will scream if he withdraws now. I will claw at his skin. I will wail like... well... me.*

"Of course, I want to bloody well finish it," I add, and this time, I do roll my eyes. "Do it, Luc. I dare you."

It's childish, certainly, but it gets the job done. His groan morphs into a yell and he thrusts again, only this time it is desire that blasts through my system rather than pain. I drop my hands from his shoulders and clutch at his perfectly shaped butt, urging him closer, deeper and faster. My legs coil around his waist, ankles pressing into his lower back, locking him in place. He complies, ratcheting up the rhythm until nothing exists but the relentless bang, bang, bang into my receptive body. I squeeze my legs to meet each thrust, my grip around his hips as tight as it can be. It feels right, clinging to him like a limpet, urging him deeper again. My breath rasps noisily as he rides my body, and I gasp and moan and beg for him to finish.

"Aleah, I can't do this...I can't wait any—"

"*Come!*" I shout the word as loudly as it is possible for me to do with my faulty voice. I don't want him to tell me all the things he can't do. I want him to focus on *this*. On *us*.

He does, letting loose with a roar and emptying into me with a rush of what feels like liquid heat somewhere deep inside my womb. The pumping motion, the slick wetness, the sound of his moaning voice and my continued gasps as our bodies slap, slap, slap against each other—all of these things together tip me over the edge once again. Only this time, the orgasm starts from deep within and is just as powerful as the first.

I scream and lose myself in the myriad of sensation, bucking and moaning beneath him until there's nothing left but *this*. Luc and I, together. As one. Eventually, after what seems like aeons, I drift back to the here and now. He strokes my cheek and stares at me with what appears to be dazed confusion.

"What?" I ask.

He's still seated inside me. It's ridiculous in this moment to be embarrassed by his intent scrutiny, but I am.

I shift, uncomfortable with his unmoving gaze.

"Do not move... just yet."

My eyes widen. "Are you okay?"

"Just sensitive."

"Hmm." I look away. I can still feel him watching me. "What?"

"Nothing." He doesn't sound perturbed in the slightest by my tone. Always cool, calm, and collected, even now. "Just...taking in your beauty."

"Oh. Well, thanks."

Luc is *nothing* like I expected. Joy rises in me. Perhaps I did make the right decision to finally give up my long-held virginity to this man. Perhaps I should listen to gut instinct more often.

"You always smell like honey," he continues. His

hand reaches up and pushes away stray strands of hair currently matted to my face. "Sweet and pure. I love it."

"Well, thank you." I clear my throat and begin to trace circles on his shoulder. "Again. The bees are my passion. I guess I just carry their scent with me wherever I go."

"And it is *delectable*." His voice is almost a purr and my toes curl in response. "So subtle as to be almost not there. Divine. It gets inside my head until I can't think properly."

"Oh." I need more than just a one-word response. "Is that a good thing?"

"Depends on the circumstances of the moment and whether I need to keep my wits about me, I suppose," he says. "Right now, it's a very good thing."

His free hand mimics my action and begins to trace lazy patterns across my naked breasts. He then drifts downward to explore lower, where our bodies still remain joined.

I can't help the surprised puff of breath that escapes. Seems I've not had enough of Luc. His caress intensifies, feather-light and yet insistent, until the ache in my clit reaches unbearable levels.

His hand movements quicken and a fingertip slides past my clit to explore the wetness of my seam that still holds his own organ captive. A low rumble starts up in his chest.

"Yes. *Oh!* You really do have very skilful...fingers." Shivers run through me and the desire seats completely in the region he's exploring. My lady parts are heavy and full and achy.

"I do," he agrees. If I wasn't so consumed by pleasure, I probably would call out his arrogance. But I cannot focus on anything except his touch.

He shifts suddenly, rolling sideways and taking me over with him until he's lying on his back and I have no choice but to sit straddling his hips. His erection is once again at full mast; I feel its length and girth deep inside, pushing at the walls of my channel. I pause, giving myself time to adjust with him so deeply buried inside of me. Being on top feels different, but in a good way. I rock gently back and forth, experimenting a little, and we both release a low moan in unison.

Well, that works. That works very nicely, indeed.

It amazes me that there are so many different ways to experience pleasure with the same person.

"And you have a very skilful...*body*." His voice is a rasp. I have no idea how he still has the ability to talk at all, especially when he fills me up in all the right places.

His captivating eyes are half-closed as he urges my hips to continue their leisurely sway. His fangs are out and their sharp whiteness against his darker lips doesn't scare me as much as it did when I first caught a glimpse of the predator on my doorstep.

I lean forward and press my lips to his, exploring a little and swiping the toothy protrusions with my tongue, all the while keeping my hip movement going, back and forth, as my clit enjoys its own pleasure against his groin.

My gestures are all instinctual. I just keep doing what feels good.

The resultant groan from Luc is deep and hoarse. "God, Aleah. I can't seem to get enough of you."

"I know that feeling."

This time, our coupling is much slower and gentler. I sink into a hot mess of need and rising desire as time ceases to exist. *I* cease to exist. There's only Luc's mouth beneath mine, unhurried movements deep within my body, and heat that sears like a rush of wildfire along my veins.

When the slow build reaches its crescendo, I lose control with a muted shriek. I climax around him, my channel clenching and unclenching as I shudder and collapse onto his chest. The sensation dims briefly and then reignites, over and over. The ecstasy continues on and on until there's nothing left but a mighty roar from Luc as he, too, falls over the edge into orgasm. We shudder and shake together until our bodies sink into an exhausted sleep. This time, coming back from oblivion takes much longer.

When I open my eyes and meet Luc's gaze, he smiles. There isn't an ounce of the predator left in that smile. It softens his features, giving the impression of someone younger and less jaded than what I'm used to seeing. I like this new version of Luc. I want to see more of him.

"I do have one question." He shifts a lock of hair off my face, the touch like a zap of electricity.

"Mmm?"

I think this must be what they call the after-glow. Whatever it is, it's upon me. I slide off him until we're lying side by side. I would be happy to keep drifting in the warmth until we gently sink back into sleep, but he props himself up on one elbow and stares down with an intent look.

"What do you do with all the honey?"

Laughter bubbles up. "*That's* your post-sex question?"

"I'm curious."

"I keep some for myself." My lips part involuntarily as he traces my jawline, and his eyes narrow in obvious satisfaction at my reaction. "I...*oh!*"

His hand circles my nipples and they pucker in response. He gives me another self-satisfied, narrow-eyed look.

"That's...um...I also create other products like candles and beeswax furniture polish and soap, and sell some at... at the local craft shop in town...That feels very nice, Luc."

How is it possible that I can still crave more? How is it possible that I haven't slid into the abyss, broken in two, and can still handle another round?

"Good." He grins, tracing a figure eight around my breasts.

I remember his bite and quickly look down, but

cannot see any mark whatsoever around either of my nipples. "You did...bite me, didn't you? I didn't imagine that?"

"I most certainly did, and it was delicious." He flicks one of the peaked nubs playfully. "My saliva has healing properties, if I choose to allow it. I could drink my fill of you every evening and no one would ever see a mark."

"Hmm." *Not sure how I feel about that. Every night? Might be a bit much.* My traitorous clit throbs delightfully at the thought of Luc and I doing *this*, every night. It's as if my body wishes to prove my brain wrong.

He splays his fingers over my ribs. "You have such a beautiful body, Aleah. Perfect in every way. What happened to your voice? Why is it—"

"Defective?"

"Well, I wouldn't go so far as—"

"I would. And it is. I don't know." I shrug, the lifelong frustration eating away at me. I don't like talking about it. I don't like that he's noticed it and brings it up because it reminds me of something I don't want to talk about. But I find myself sharing my story, and it is easier to share with him than I thought. "I guess I was just born with a voice that is difficult to hear, especially when it matters most."

Luc frowns. "Is there anything you can do, though? Even if the dying—or their families—*could* hear you, there's nothing a banshee can do to prevent death coming. Is there?"

"I don't *know*!" That's the crux of the matter, and the reason for all of my angst. "What if there is? What if, when people hear my wail, they become more vigilant, or pick up a weapon, or...or... I don't know. Do *something* to change the outcome! What if other banshees have the power to change the course of fate?"

I sit up now, too energized to lie still. I hold the sheet against my chest, even though he has seen me, even though he's touching me. My thoughts are on my wail. If it wasn't defective, I might actually be able to help people, to warn them before death has a chance to take them.

"Don't you know?" He scoots next to me, placing his hand on my thigh. The thin material of the sheet protects me from nothing, and even though he's rather cool, warmth spreads through my body. "Can't you ask...I don't know...*someone*?"

"*Who*?" I shift with frustration and Luc removes his hand. "My mother abandoned me as a baby and I was raised by humans alone. The only things I know about *anything* fae is what I've accidentally discovered myself, or what I see or hear in the news!"

I don't realize I'm wringing my hands until Luc's come down to cover mine.

"I apologize, Aleah." His touch is cool, not cold, and the instant he cradles my clenched fists I feel butterflies start up in my belly. Light butterfly wings beating gently, lifting my energy and increasing awareness until there is nothing left but him, and me, and our connected hands resting on the coverlet. "I didn't mean to upset you. Rest now. We've expended a lot of energy this evening."

I release a sigh, trying to let go of questions that have no answer. He's right. We have expended a lot of energy.

I must fall asleep, because when I wake, Luc is leaning up on one elbow watching me. He seems to be making it a habit.

"Good morning." My greeting is automatic.

His answering grin is faintly feral, but I'm beginning to enjoy rather than recoil from that hint of the predatory in his nature.

"*Almost* morning," he corrects, his voice husky with sleep. "I'll need to leave soon, before dawn breaks."

Part of me doesn't want him to leave.

"Before you do, where are you from, Luc?" I sit up, brushing the hair that falls in his face. I'm trying to keep him here, delay his trip. "I mean, originally? What's your background?"

He raises one dark eyebrow. "Well, you already know I was born in France." He sits on the edge of the bed, indulging me, for which I'm grateful. "I lived in Paris until the age of thirty-six, when I was turned by a Parisian courtesan who I...*uh*..." The rush of sadness that chokes his voice is unexpected.

"A woman you loved?"

"Yeah. I *did* love Veronique. I loved her before she turned me, and I loved her until the day she met her true death." He plays with the edge of the coverlet, until the fidgeting becomes too much.

This time it is I who covers his hand to force stillness. I don't like hearing about someone he used to care for, and yet, I'm glad he shared that knowledge with me. I appreciate his trust.

Eventually he continues. "I stayed a while with my Maker and her clan, until..."

Pain flares briefly in his features before quickly being masked.

"Until?" My prompt is gentle.

"Until her death by stake many years ago." The admission is stilted. Whoever Veronique was to Luc in life, or after his turning, he clearly loved her dearly. I'm surprised to find I'm not terribly threatened by this admission. I've never loved anyone as fiercely as he clearly loved her. I don't know if I ever will.

The mention of a stake reminds me I need to replenish the one that normally resides in my belt loop. Luc may have proven not to be a threat, but that doesn't mean all vamps have suddenly become angels in training.

When I'm in the throes of a death call, my mind is fuzzy and I need the comforting protection a stake can bring. Perhaps I make some kind of move or telling gesture, because he nods toward my dresser.

"They're all in there, ready for you to sheathe and

strap back on. When you do use the weapon, grip it like *this* rather than the way you held it when you were facing me." He does some complicated movement with his fingers, mimicking a slightly different hold for the stake than the one I would normally use. "If you hold it like *this*, you'll have more control. It'll be easier to strike *here*..." He touches the soft 'v' at the base of his throat. "Or the eye, or even into his ear if he's not facing forward. Or here." He indicates the groin area. "And whatever you do, Allie, strike to kill. You'll only have one chance."

It's strange to watch him teach me how to kill him, if I choose. The fact that we're both still naked just adds to the unusualness of the situation. And yet, it doesn't feel wrong.

I nod without speaking. I hope it will never come to that, though I'm damn sure not going to leave home without my stakes now. Nor the silver knife. Not after what has been happening out there.

He studies me for a moment and adds a last piece of advice. "With the current situation, might not hurt to add one of those silver daggers to your arsenal—at least until every rogue is disabled and we've gotten to the bottom of what's really going on."

"Are you a mind reader, now?" I slide out of bed and head over to the dresser. I open the drawer to see what I have available.

"Not really," he says. He gestures with his chin. "But your fingers clench in a particular way when you're about to hold your stake. I noticed it that first night—and you just did the same thing again a few moments earlier."

Heat warms my cheeks and I'm glad I'm not looking at him directly. "It's not you," I tell him. I'm surprised that I actually mean it. "It's just…I'm sorry. My experience of vamps is limited and what I do know of them…of your kind…is not pleasant."

I swallow. My throat is dry. How have I changed this much in so little time? Apologizing for something I used to be so sure of.

"You said one ruined your life." His voice is tentative. "You were attacked?"

"No." I shake my head, deciding on a stake and pulling it out. "It was my father. He…he died. I was four." My eyes narrow on the stake as I twist it in my hand, trying out the hold Luc suggested. The action is easier than remembering.

"Oh, Aleah. I'm so very sorry. It must have been a young vamp, freshly turned, perhaps, and temporarily hunger-driven." He's trying to be nice, but it doesn't help. I don't want to hear about how it's a tragic accident that shouldn't have happened in the first place. "Those of us older and more experienced will feed without harming our prey. As you experienced last night."

Prey. What am I thinking, entertaining such a being in my bed? He sees all human creatures as his prey, obviously including me.

I slam the drawer shut and turn to face him. My tone is sharper than I intend when I answer. "It wasn't a young vamp. It was two of them. And one was actually a woman."

Luc stands up so quickly I don't even see the movement. His eyes narrow. "A...*woman*?"

Why is he surprised by that news? I nod, gripping my stake tightly in my hand. I know Luc won't attack me, but I feel much safer holding onto it compared to when I didn't. "Yes, that's what my aunt told me, when I grew old enough to understand."

"I...see." There's a new note of tension in his tone. I'm not sure what it means. "If you were four, then this was about twenty-five years ago?"

"Mm hmm. What's the matter?" I narrow my eyes, sitting a safe distance away from him on the bed.

"I'm not sure." There's a note in his voice I can't identify. "Have you always lived in Hatton Grove?"

What a strange question. "No. I was born in the city, and lived in Melbourne with my aunt after my father passed away." I suddenly feel naked in front of him, exposed, and want to cover up. I'm not ashamed of my body, but it's deeper than just my physical appearance. "It was only after she died too—cancer, sadly—that I decided to get away from...people."

Luc's frown creates vertical lines between his dark brows.

"So, you moved here because of your gift?" he asks.

A *gift*. No one has ever suggested my banshee power is anything but a curse.

I nearly laugh but stop myself. I go back to my dresser and this time pull out some underwear.

"Yes, it is a little easier out here," I say. "I don't experience every human death. If I did, it would be non-stop agony and I think perhaps that would kill me, too, despite the protection afforded by my fae blood. I do feel the call if it occurs within a certain proximity. I might be isolated from others out here, but where there are less people, there are less death calls."

Until the rogues came to town.

As if he hears my last thought, Luc runs his fingers through his hair.

"I need to check out some information," he says in a rush. "I have to go, Aleah, and I'm not sure when I'll return."

Oh. Well. That was over quick. Why am I not surprised?

"Sure."

At my core, I know he genuinely has to leave, especially given the nature of his job and the threat we're currently facing in this area. But the sudden need to exit dredges up past not-so-enjoyable memories. It has been three years since I moved here and started tending my precious bees. Three and a half since my last "almost" hook-up with a man who got to witness first-hand the anguish of a banshee's death call. We were just about to get hot and heavy when the agony hit. I will never forget the look of horror and disgust on his face as death came for one of my fellow tenants in the apartment building.

"You're one of *those*? A *supernatural creature*? I thought you were like me. Human."

He spat on me and left, and I couldn't even muster the energy to wipe off his spittle because I was curled up on the floor of my apartment in the throes of death, wailing softly to myself.

That was not my first experience of *speciesism*, which is what the blind hatred of anyone or anything not human is called under Accord rules. Back then, though, it was the final catalyst to sell up and move out here where there is less chance to experience the call of the banshee.

It's probably one of the reasons why I haven't gone out of my way to look for another hook-up since then. The last thing I need is a repeat experience of that humiliation.

Luc finishes dressing and pauses at the door. "I would stay if I could, little one," he says, his tone genuine. "Our story has only just begun. I *will* return."

There's so much promise in his tone my body heats once again. Visions of all the ways he could take me flash across my mind like a movie.

Of course, he picks up on it. Why would he not? He's a vamp with heightened senses. His nostrils flare, as if he can smell my need from all the way across the room.

"Have a shower, Aleah," he says. "Wash off the residue of our lovemaking and enjoy all the nuances of sensation that your no-longer-virginal body will now reveal. I will leave a pot of coffee for you downstairs."

Such a mundane way to finish, and yet he puts so much subtle inference into the words that a shiver runs all the way from my scalp to my toes. Is it because he's a supe that my whole body feels energized and full of zing? Is it because of his vampirism, calling to my hybrid blood and speeding up my pulse to breakneck speed?

Or is it as simple as pheromones and nothing at all to do with species? A man and a woman, whose chemistry calls to each other in a way I never knew existed outside of romance books. Whatever it is, I can't wait for his eventual return.

My body aches in unfamiliar places and I need to take Luc's advice and have a shower to wash away the remaining traces of mine and the vampire's coupling.

The hot water meanders down my body. What would it be like to have his hands follow the rivulets of moisture over my curves? My nipples harden at the thought, and the nub between my legs swells in anticipation of a caress that I pray might eventuate again.

Even though we spent most of the night making love, it seems my body has still not had enough. I wasn't sure what I expected, but it definitely wasn't this. I feel alive, like a whole new world has opened up to me.

The sun is high in the sky when I finally make my way downstairs and add some bread to the toaster. Where is he sheltering now that it's full daylight? Is he back at the Royal Hotel, in his presumably daylight-proof room? I know most hotels these days offer rooms specially fitted out for any supernatural clientele, but until now I'd never thought about it in the context of my local pub and eating place. Hopefully he has gone to ground, wherever he might be. Even though it's mid-winter, the weather has been unseasonably warm and there's a bite in the sun when it's out, even for non-vampires like myself.

In some respects, it is good that he decided to leave now. The distress and distraction of the past couple of days has taken over and I need to check on my bees. I haven't been out to the hives recently and I have to collect honey and wax and head into town to replenish some of the wares in the shop. Hopefully, that will give me a chance to find out about funeral arrangements for Darrie and Gwen.

After breakfast, I don protective wear and head out to the far paddock with my smoker and collection tub to check the hives. I never take too much—the honey provides sustenance for the bees as much as it does for my customers and I would never deprive them of what my babies need to thrive.

The swarm is buzzing with more activity than

usual. Most are usually out collecting at this time. The mood is so agitated I need to add smoke to calm them down. Usually I can just croon to them in my defective voice, which for some strange reason they seem to love. I bring the smoker only as a precaution, but this is the first time since I began keeping bees that I've been forced to use it.

What is going on? A glance around the field reveals no sign that anyone else has been here, and the hives certainly look untouched, but something has unsettled them.

Afterward, I visit the storage barn that serves as my warehouse, and load up my car with the latest batch of honey-based products I finished making last week. Sales of these products via the local store in town is how I make enough to pay the bills. It's not much, but I live simply. Once the car is loaded up, I head into Hatton Grove for my usual fortnightly visit.

Laura, the woman who owns the store, is standing behind the register, adding price tickets to a pile of items on the counter. She greets me with a worried look instead of her usual smile.

"How are you doing, Aleah?" she asks. "I'm really concerned about you out there on your own. I heard about Darrie and Gwen."

"Yes, such a terrible thing." We hug for longer than usual. Eventually we release each other. "Do you know anything about the funeral, Laura?"

"It won't be for a little while, I believe," she says,

brushing her bangs out of her face. "I think there's something about their deaths that needs further investigation. We all thought some kind of wild animal when we first heard, but Bernie said the supe police are now involved, so you know what *that* means."

My heart thumps as I nod. Word certainly gets around quickly in small towns. Bernie, our local cop, should know better than to spread gossip, but I guess everyone is worried about their own family and friends as well as being sad for the loss of such a popular local couple.

"I think they found something at the scene," Laura continues. "Bernie started to say, but then he bit his tongue and refused to speak about it further."

What did they find? Does Luc know about this? What does it mean?

Before I can ask any questions out loud, Laura lays a hand on my forearm. "Are you all right out there on your own, Allie? You can always come and stay at ours for a bit, if you like. You know Davey loves to see you."

I smile at Laura, grateful for her caring attitude. "Davey is adorable, and you know I love him." Laura's seven-year-old son has Down syndrome, and I don't think I've ever met a sweeter child. Like my dear neighbors, Davey and Laura are among the small handful of people I've allowed in close to my heart. I couldn't bear it if anything happened to them as well. "Thank you for the offer, hon, but I'll be fine. I'm used to taking care of myself."

She frowns, but lets it drop for now. For that, I'm grateful. I head back out to the car and start unloading trays of new product for the store. I have a new range of candles made with beeswax and a batch of honey-fragranced soap that has proven popular with tourists passing through the region.

After I drop off my wares, I head to the store to stock up on groceries and cat food. Everywhere I visit, the mood is somber. Everyone is talking about my neighbors and making wild guesses about what might really have happened. I hear talk of vampires, werewolves, maybe a bear shifter, and even demons reaching up from the depths of hell to rip out their hearts and eat them. At least one of those guesses is correct, but preternatural creatures these days are mostly as respecting of human life as any human, and no one really has a handle on exactly what happened and why.

Luc's name is bandied about here or there, too. The townsfolk seem particularly fascinated by the sexy vampire cop who has breezed into town to save us all. At least, that's the gist of the various chats at the grocery store, where I fill my cart with supplies for the next fortnight and eavesdrop on snippets of conversation.

"Have you seen him? Sexy as hell, with that black hair and those piercing blue eyes."

"Can you imagine being seduced by a man who looks like that?"

"Better than my old hubby, any day."

"I would do him, even if he is a vampire. Hell, if he's good, I may even let him bite me."

Titters of laughter fade away, and I'm left alone with images of what it actually *did* feel like to be seduced by Luc. I want to call out and let them know that when he's in the throes of passion, his eyes turn green instead of blue, so green that it feels as if you could dive in so deep you might never find your way back out.

Instead, I bite my tongue and let the other women drift away, and carry my bags back to the car to begin the return trek to the farm.

I hope, wherever Luc is, that he's okay. And I hope that, tonight, when he's at peak strength, he'll finally manage to find and destroy the remaining loup. I miss my town of tension-free, easy-to-talk-to people. At least Luc gives them a nice distraction. I can't fault their attraction to him. I feel the same way.

When I get home and begin to unpack, I realize there's a note stuck on my coffee maker. He must have written it in the early hours of the morning before he left. I'm not sure how I missed it earlier.

Be careful, little banshee. The rogue attacks are indiscriminate and are clearly focused in this area, at least for the present. I won't stop until I have tracked him down and ended his deadly spree. I can't remain here to protect you and hunt at the same time. I will be back as soon as I can.

I scowl at the patronizing tone of the note.

"I never asked you to stay and protect me." I say the words out loud, even though there's no one bar my two cats to hear. It makes me feel much better, though. Maybe I've been alone for too long if talking to myself relieves my annoyance. "I don't need your protection. I don't need anyone's protection. I've done pretty well up till now looking after myself."

He has a point though, and I make a mental note to drop in to the local gun shop next time I'm in town to pick up an additional weapon. A wooden stake might be of use against a vamp, if I strike swiftly and firmly enough, but against a rabid were? I need silver protection for that. My knives upstairs might offer some defense, but they require close quarter fighting and perhaps something with silver bullets might be a better option for a confirmed non-fighter like me. I really should learn to fight at some point. I keep putting it off, even though I shouldn't, especially living alone.

The sun is low on the horizon when I head upstairs to reload my belt. A stake in the loop on the left, and a knife in the right-hand loop. From now on, whenever I head outside, I will make sure I'm ready for anything. Thank goodness for Luc's additional instruction in how best to wield a stake. I can only hope it will be enough, if I'm ever in a situation that warrants using it.

I stand at the window and scan for any sign of Luc,

but of course he's nowhere to be seen. I can't believe how quickly he managed to get under my skin.

In a million years I would never have imagined losing my virginity to a vampire, of all creatures, and yet, now that it's done, I don't regret the decision one bit. Luc intrigues me in a way I didn't expect.

My gut instinct still says he's dangerous, but not toward me. Not unless I end up on the wrong side of the law. Even then, I don't think he would harm me. There's something almost tender in his touch and in his look that I think surprises even him.

Luc is someone I'd like to spend more time with, but that's unlikely until this current situation is sorted and the danger to the community I know and love has passed.

I'M NOT sure what sound awakens me, but I come to consciousness instantly, reaching for the weaponed belt on my bedside table.

Bobo is sitting up on the bed, all bristled and bushy-looking. Suki is on the dresser, and even in the darkness I note her wide-eyed alertness. Both are staring toward the window.

I slide out of bed, thankful I fell asleep wearing a t-shirt and pajama bottoms instead of my usual nakedness. The belt fits neatly around my waist and I slip my feet into a pair of boots sitting by the door. If I have to venture outside, I need to be mindful of snakes on top of any supernatural creatures who might be lurking in the vicinity, though admittedly it would be rare to encounter a snake at this colder time of the year.

The cats crowd my legs as I creep down the stairs, and then both of them disappear under the nearest furniture when we reach the base. What has the cats so spooked? My heart pounds fast and my breath is shallow.

Once in the kitchen, I stare out through the screen door into the night, leaving my lights off and waiting for my eyes to adjust. I search for any unusual movement along the tree line edging the garden area. Nothing. What woke me? What has caused these goose bumps to raise up along my arms?

Something is going on, something I can't quite put my finger on, and I don't like it. There's a prickle in the air that just feels...*wrong*. But even with my fae-enhanced vision I can't discern anything out of the ordinary.

I'm just about to turn away when the sound of a car careening madly up the road fills the air. It turns in to my property and comes to a screeching halt right at my garden gate.

Laura? When my friend opens the door and lurches out, I realize she's bleeding from some kind of facial wound. My eyes widen. *What the actual hell?*

I yank open the kitchen door and race down the

stairs to meet her. She opens the rear passenger door of the car and my heart lurches when she pulls her young son, Davey, from the back seat. He's as pale as a ghost, his dark eyes large and frightened.

"Let us in. Let us in. Aleah, please help us." Laura is sobbing, and reaches out toward me with one hand while clutching at Davey with the other.

Both of them collapse into my arms and Laura begins to cry in earnest. The boy is silent, clearly too traumatized to make any sound. I stagger under the weight but then right myself, lifting Davey onto one hip and supporting my friend as I make soothing noises and try to calm them both down.

"Shh. It's okay, you're here now." I begin to lead them inside, slowly at first. They're already spooked enough. I don't want to rush them, but I also don't want to remain out here, like sitting ducks. "What happened, hon? Come on inside. Do you need me to call an ambulance? Is Davey okay? Are you—"

"They nearly got him," she says. She continues to move toward the house, but I can tell she's in a daze, as though not quite sure how she managed to survive. "They nearly got Dave. But I grabbed one of grandma's silver knives and..."

They? She gulps and starts crying again, and fear crashes into me when I realize what must have happened. *Silver. A supe.* All humans keep silver now, since the preternaturals came out of hiding. Silver won't kill a vamp the way it will a shifter, but it will slow down any supernatural creature except fae. Iron is a fae's weakness, and even though my human blood enables me to tolerate it, even I avoid touching anything iron more than I have to.

"Come on." I rub her shoulder as we make it to the door. "It's okay. Let's get you both inside."

I guide them toward the stairs.

A low growl comes from behind us.

Oh. Shit.

My heart lurches in my throat. That growl is not natural. None of the animals who roam these farms would create such a sound. Which means that whatever attacked Laura and her son has followed them here.

I need to get them inside, and quickly.

I lean in to Laura and whisper, "Get inside now, and lock the door. Call Bernie at the station and tell him the rogue vamp is here. Tell them to find the vampire cop and let him know the loup is at Aleah's place. *Go.*"

I push at the two of them, trying to emphasize my point. Why will they not move faster?

"But how will you—"

"*Quickly!*" I nod at her son. "Think of Davey."

I don't wait to see if she has complied. Instead, I turn and scan the darkness in the direction of the sound.

Yes, *there.* A set of eerily-red eyes stares unblinkingly in my direction. I have two choices. I can back up, slowly, and try to make it up the stairs and all the way inside to safety before he charges. It's still possible I might make it before he can cross the yard and reach me. I *might*. Or, I can stand and fight for the people I care about.

If I can hold him off long enough for the cops to get here—long enough for Luc to get here, is what I really mean, and this moment behoves self-honesty—then they might have a chance to bring him down instead of endlessly chasing a shadowy will-o-the-wisp who always lives to kill another day.

Keep him here long enough for Luc to arrive and help me save the day. A little voice inside my head starts laughing maniacally at that thought. He's not going to get here before I'm torn to shreds like my unfortunate neighbors. No one is going to get here in time.

What good are you, dead, to anyone? Running is the best option. Run. A glance over my shoulder reveals that Laura and Davey are now safely under my roof. He won't get them now, not unless they venture back outside. Despite the fact that he's a rogue, I'm banking on the fact that he still can't get into my home without an invitation.

An image of my dad rises in my memory. The two of us are seated at the kitchen table, both laughing as he pulls a ridiculous face and three-year-old me tries to mimic him. My father, so loving and supportive even though his daughter was different than everyone else we knew.

I failed him back then. And while I will likely die trying tonight, there's no way I can run from this. Part of me wishes Luc were here right now, so we could fight together and have half a chance. Part of me is utterly terrified, knowing that tonight's the night I'm probably going to die.

But the part of me that wins the argument is the one that says, *enough. No more.* I have had enough of rogue supes who go around killing innocent people.

The vamp moves out of the trees into the clearing and I finally get my first real look at the monster of my nightmares. This is no Luc. This creature is naked, its whole body white and hunched, with long, spindly limbs reminiscent of a spider. Its face is frozen in a rictus of hatred. The red glow of his eyes is freakishly scary and the spittle dripping off his yellowish fangs makes my stomach turn. There's no smell, as such, but there's an oozing oily miasma of something poisonous surrounding him that just feels *wrong.*

Chapter Eight

My fae half senses that this is no ordinary rogue. The creature carries some unnamed darkness within him that no amount of "loupness" can explain.

Intelligence flares behind the red glow and that fact in itself is far more frightening than all the rest put together. Loups *have* no reason. Loups do not think logically and rationally—which means this creature is dangerous.

And I've chosen to remain outside and face him. *Idiot. Please let the cops get here soon. Please let Luc get here in time.*

My heart pounds so hard it feels like it's about to lurch right up out of my chest. For a moment, I think my legs might fail me. I lock my knees to hold myself upright. I will not fall in front of this devil creature. I will not die on my knees without first putting up a damn good fight. If I fail—and there's a good chance I will—I want to make damn sure this creature thinks twice before attacking again. I want him to remember the fight I put up and to ask himself if he really wants to risk death.

At least I was able to save them. I couldn't save Darrie or Gwen. I couldn't save my beloved dad. But I'm damn sure going to do my best to enable Davey and Laura to live through this nightmare and see the light of tomorrow.

Thank everything that's holy I brought my weapons out here with me, though carrying one measly little knife and a wooden stick to this fight will be like trying to subdue a tiger with a toothpick. Still, my odds are better than Laura's, and I don't have something that can be used against me. I don't have a child.

"Come on, you crazy, naked little vamp. Want to play? Try me." *What the fuck am I doing?* He has already proven insane. He won't need me to taunt him any further to get him to attack.

Do banshees ever herald their own impending death?

I don't know enough about my own kind. I hid from my heritage all these years because I was scared of it, and now I won't get to explore who I really am. I don't know how things might have progressed with Luc, if we'd only had the chance. Now I'll never know.

I haven't lived long enough to die tonight.

I shift the stake to rest more comfortably in my

grip, exactly the way Luc showed me, and draw the knife with my other hand. I feel safer with these weapons in my hands, even if they are miniscule. Even if they end up not making a difference. Then a tiny yelp escapes me when another set of red eyes appears beside the first.

Two of them.

Laura said *they* almost got Davey. *They*. *Fuck it*. I'm facing down not one, but two crazed rogues.

Is there a fucking loup factory near here? As one goes down, another steps up to take its place?

This second one is no vamp. His maw is huge and distended, and filled with slavering teeth. Unlike the skinny vamp, his body is stocky and muscled. Half human, half furred werewolf. Another fucking were. Where does this vamp find his friends? Some kind of deadly zoo?

The were doesn't need my permission to enter my home and reach my friends. As that realization sinks in, the vamp attacks.

He launches in a blur I can barely see. I call on everything fae within me to rise to the surface and help. *Fae blood. Bring me strength. Bring me speed. Bring me luck. Please.* I slash blindly outward with the stake, side-stepping just in time. A rage-filled hiss in my ear and the lightest of grazes on my neck indicate how close I just came to having my throat torn out. Wetness coats my skin. Is it blood? Did he nick me? Or is it spittle that dripped from those disgusting yellow incisors?

No time to check. The weight of his charge knocks me onto my back and takes the breath completely from my lungs. I can't see the were from this position, not with the vampire hunched on top of me, staring down into my face. My arms are pinned to my side by his bony knees. No way to use the weapons I brought. No way to protect myself. I'm helpless and there's nothing I can do about it.

His mouth widens into an evil grin and I have to fight the urge to vomit as a trail of saliva dribbles out and drops onto my cheek. It's warm and slimy on my flesh.

"You want to play, hybrid?" The words are deep and gravelly—as if drawn from the depths of some unknown hell rather than emanating from his actual being. "Then why not tell me your name?"

He wants my name? A strange request. My lungs finally begin to recover from being winded. Enough that I manage to draw in a breath and spit up into his face, but he only cocks his head and laughs. Horror rolls over me at the cracked sound. *Is this the last thing I will hear? Is this the last thing I will feel—this spindly devil's weight pressing me down into the damp night earth?*

I start to wiggle underneath him. I may be incapacitated but I refuse to let that stop me trying.

I blink away sudden tears as the other one appears in my vision. His wolf-like features with the red-tinged eyes above that misshapen muzzle are equally as terrifying as the vamp. He leans eagerly over the two of us, as if a spectator at a sporting event. A fight-to-the-death sporting event.

"Leave some for me." The words that emanate from the were are distorted but not to the point I can't understand him. How do these starkly different creatures have the capacity to work together?

The vamp grabs my throat and squeezes.

I want you dead, monster. I want you both dead. I can't speak out loud, not with his grip tightening around my neck until my eyes feel as if they're about to pop out of my head. The inside of my throat burns. The hum in my ears grows, overtaking all other noise.

It sounds like my bees, but that can't be right. It's night time and they're safely tucked up in their hives. Red tinges my vision and everything begins to blur. *No oxygen. Can't...breathe.*

My head is light, spinning but I'm not dizzy. I squeeze my fingers and remember I have weapons. I am not completely helpless. It's difficult to move, but if I don't, I'm dead.

Somehow, I manage to flex one of my wrists, the only part of my arm I can move, and jab into the vamp's thigh with the knife. It isn't much, but in this pinned-down state, it's the only action I can take. The tip of the silver blade is super-sharp and pierces the monster's skin deeply enough to elicit a squeal. It won't stop him for long, but the grip on my throat eases and the weight on my chest disappears. I roll away and stumble to my feet, coughing and spluttering and trying to get my crushed throat to work properly.

The titter of crazed laughter from both rogues when I raise my piddly weapons in front of me generates a shiver down my spine.

"Give us your name, banshee," the were says. "If you do, we'll let you go."

Like hell you will. They're enjoying the chase, clearly feeding on my fear. They circle me, one moving clockwise, the other anti-clockwise. I pivot, unable to keep them both in view at the same time. I'm their prey, and my time is just about up. Which of them will get me first? Will they rip me in half and share the spoils?

There's a blur of movement to my right. Luc erupts out of the trees and launches into an almighty leap over the heads of the rogues. He lands neatly beside me, his snarls rivalling those of the monsters.

My body hunches over as the first signs of death begin to call. *No! No, no, no, no.*

Not tonight, not now, and not this way.

My wail rises, as stifled as always but even more so from the damage the vamp inflicted on my neck. Luc cocks his head and I realize, despite my destroyed throat, he can hear the banshee call. This time, someone hears me. The agonizing sob breaks free and I begin to wail in earnest but there's no time or space to sink into the sadness as a whole wall of pale flesh and fur, fangs and fetid breath is upon us.

The vamp dives onto Luc, somewhere off to the side. The other lands in a huge leap right on top of me. His front paws are the size of dinner plates. I topple backward and he lands heavily on my chest. Not even being winded twice in the space a few minutes can stop the call of the banshee. It's my *other*, fed by fae magic, and something completely separate to whatever it is that gives me voice and breath.

Saliva dribbles from his maw down onto my face and he leans in close and sniffs. For a second or two I wonder if I can reason with him. Most weres aren't like this. Most weres are as reasonable as any other supe. What made him turn into a monster? Then I stare deep into his eyes and know there's no reason left. This close I can't avoid the calculated madness behind those terrifying purple-red flames of rage.

Purple?

Unlike the vamp, the were stinks. I nearly hurl from the stench of rot that emanates from his mouth, and from sheer terror at the thought that I'm about to get my throat ripped out.

"Your name, hybrid?"

We're on that again?

With effort I control the wail long enough to answer. "Fuck off, puppy dog."

His growl turns to an enraged roar. I grin defiantly up into his face even as my death wail recommences.

I'm singing my own death. Am I singing my own death? Is such a thing even possible?

His jaw opens and snaps shut on my neck just as I stab the knife directly into his eye. The blade slides in easily, and I wonder if Luc will be proud of me. A whole blade of silver, right to the hilt. And I held the knife just the way he showed me.

Shock colors his furry expression. I scream for him as his limp body collapses completely onto mine and he's so heavy I can barely breathe, let alone move. Still, the banshee call goes on. There's something very wrong, though. I'm crying and wailing, wracked with pain and sadness, but no sound emerges at all.

What is going on?

I really can't catch my breath. Panic floods through me. *I can't breathe at all.* Instead I try a gasp but it's light and gurgly. I'm choking on blood—*my* blood—and more tears fall when I realize the death call is a double one.

I guess banshees can *sing their own impending death.*

He tore open my neck before he died, and I'm choking on my own blood. Sorrow builds for the future life I'll never live, for lost chances, unrequited love, unfulfilled goals and achievements. I will never find out what might have been between Luc and me. I will never have the opportunity to build a life with someone I love by my side. I will die alone, as I've lived alone most of my life. I will never know what it is to truly love and be loved.

The banshee call builds to unbearable agony in my chest. With my throat almost completely blocked, there's nowhere for the banshee cry to escape. I'm surrounded by death, covered by it, literally with this furry carcass, and now I begin to drown.

I'm drowning in your life force, Luc.

I turn my head to the side and watch him fight, wishing I could go to his aid. Luc is faster than the rogue, by a long shot, but the crazed one is driven by something more powerful even than Luc. A purplish aura surrounds them. Is that my vision failing, or is it the shadow of whatever magics are providing strength to this loup and the seemingly endless stream of others?

A vague memory surfaces from my childhood. Me, skipping down the street toward the park and reaching out toward an old man lying on one of the park benches near the swing. *Purple. He looks so pretty all coated in purple.* My father snatching me up and whisking me back home. *Never touch the purple, Aleah. Purple is bad magic. Necromancer magic.*

The purple is always something to steer clear of. And now its seedy miasma begins to swallow Luc.

I drift toward unconsciousness. It becomes harder to keep my eyes open. I try to fight it, my father's words still ringing in my ears. *Purple is bad.* Luc is surrounded by purple. He is still a blur of movement, and I think maybe one of them is down. *Oh my God, it's Luc. Not you too. Please.*

Help him.

In the murky dark amidst the depths of the banshee death agony, I start to hallucinate. A swarm of bees rises up out of the forest and heads toward me. The humming sound in my ears increases. It can't be my bees. It's night time. My beautiful creatures, come to say good bye, at least in my imagination. I smile at the swarm, even though I know it isn't real. *Save him. Save Luc. Too late for me...*

I try with one last effort to heave off the carcass in an attempt to do something...anything...to help. *At least it won't get Laura or Davey. At least I know they're safe.*

Random thoughts...

Now the were is dead, the vamp won't be able to get in the house.

Fading...

Hey, vamp monster, look over here. Look at me. Let Luc defeat you while you're distracted.

Instead, the darkness grows, and at the last, before it takes me completely, I realize death is not so bad, after all. There's a growing warmth, a sinking feeling, and then...nothing.

Chapter Nine

LUC

She's dead. They killed her. They killed her before I had the chance to explain and beg forgiveness. I can't believe she's gone. *Aleah. Don't be gone. I need you alive.*

The loup is on top of me. I twist my head, searching for Aleah, and gravel digs into my cheek. I scrabble in the dirt, struggling in vain to throw off the weight of the monster on my chest. His rabid strength is beyond anything I've ever experienced in a vamp. He's readying for the death bite, the incisors fully extended, and I have one last chance to do this. I lay still, gather my strength, drawing upon every ounce I have. Everything I am, everything I was, and everything I might yet be, coalesces into this one, single moment of truth.

"You have no idea who you're up against. Join our cause, and I can promise you power beyond your wildest dreams." It may be the rogue speaking, but the voice isn't his. The authority emanating from the words feels ancient and strong, far older than this vamp will ever be.

A purple haze obscures my vision and I blink, trying to retain my senses. When my vision clears, I see a medallion at the creature's neck. A medallion that looks exactly like the one I found at Aleah's neighbor's farm.

"Who are you?" I ask. This feels both familiar and strange to me.

The rogue grins widely, baring his fangs at me. I snarl straight back at him. *See? My fangs are bigger than your yellow, rotten teeth.*

"I am the one who will lead the Restoration. Restore the balance of power to where it should be. Give us her true name, descendent of *Dracule*, and you will bask in the glory alongside the supreme ones."

Give us her name? My snarl intensifies as I continue to gather my strength. A strange buzzing in my ears deepens. It's now or never. I take a breath to steady myself, timing my moment, readying to twist this fucker's head right off his shoulders.

Instead, my mouth drops open and I involuntarily freeze as a swarm of bees descends out of nowhere and coats every exposed inch of the rogue's lily-white skin.

His screech of rage and shock is suddenly cut off as more bees fly into his open mouth. I snap mine shut, though the bees seem to be completely ignoring me and targeting only the rogue.

Bee stings won't kill him, of course, but this many in such a coordinated attack disable him long enough that I'm able to achieve the impossible.

Aleah's bees. She's saving my life yet again.

I switch off further thought and reach into the swarm, finding the loup's ears. He scratches toward me. Using his ears as leverage, I twist violently with every bit of stored strength I have. His head rips apart from the neck. It holds together by a stubborn piece of the spinal column. With an extra yank I snap that too, then toss the head aside and roll the now-sagging carcass off me. Bees continue to swarm all over it, the angry buzz so loud I can't hear anything above the noise.

There's no time to consider why the swarm only targeted the rogue, and whether or not they'll go after me next. I sprint to Aleah's side and drop to my knees beside her. An involuntary moan escapes my lips when I see the amount of blood that has already seeped into the ground. Her throat is a mess, her beautiful face so white she almost shines luminescent in the moonlight.

She's non-responsive, but as a vamp I *feel* her pulse still beating, even without having to reach out and search for it. It's faint, but there. She's still alive, albeit barely hanging on by a thread.

I nearly let out a sob. I can't believe she's alive. I can't believe...but I need to focus. I need to figure out how to help her. I have no idea whether her fae blood will protect her from death.

"Allie." I dip my fingertip in the open flesh wound of her neck.

She doesn't stir. Her blood is calling to the vamp in me, desperately screaming, but I ignore the call. *This is Aleah.* The one I want to protect more than anyone in this world. And I've failed her. I've failed.

"*Aleah!*" This time I yell her name into the breeze. When did she become so important to me? I've known her scant days, and yet, her death seems unthinkable. I can't bear the thought of a world without her in it.

I need to do *something*. But what?

A rush of latent energy washes through the air. I jump to my feet, not knowing what is happening but determined to protect Aleah. I stand over her broken body and growl.

A tall faerie woman in a long, pale blue dress appears in the clearing, staring at us. She has the same hair and facial features as Allie, but there's a cold, translucent quality about this woman that denotes full fae, and a powerful one, at that.

"My daughter's blood has been spilt. *My* blood." She strides toward us, her mouth twisting as she stares down at Aleah. "What have you done this time, vampire? How many fae...how many humans...must die before the abominations are stopped?"

I ignore her question. "Can you help her? Can you save her? Is it too late..."

She kneels beside her daughter's broken body and runs her hands over Allie from her head to her toes, stopping to dip her fingers into the blood that layers the ground around her neck. "Far too late, if she stays here even a minute longer. If I take her home with me—"

"You mean, to the fae realm?"

"Of course." She looks at me as though I am nothing more than dirt beneath her shoe.

Under normal circumstances, my pride would prickle and I would attempt to put this fae in her place. With Aleah's life hanging in the balance, I ignore her withering glare.

"If I don't, I will shortly be singing in the death of my own child. I may still have to do that, regardless. *Hurry*." She calls out loudly in a language I don't understand, and out of a sudden silver mist another fae appears. A large man, in dark armor, who bends and lifts Aleah into his arms. "Take her straight to my quarters, Tarrien, and commence without me. Go."

And just like that, Aleah is gone.

The faerie woman straightens and meets my narrowed gaze.

"I recognize you, vampire," she says. "I know you were there at the death of my daughter's father. Have you told her the role you played?"

My heart lurches in shock. I clench my teeth, and then look away.

"Not yet," I admit. "I planned to, though I haven't had the chance—"

"Now you never will." Her voice is steely, leaving no room for argument. "Farewell."

She turns away.

"Wait!"

Perhaps she can hear real desperation in my tone because she pauses and briefly turns back to face me.

"It—whatever it was—wanted her true name. It's not Aleah, I take it?"

Shock ripples across her features and the misty aura surrounding her changes from silver to gray-green and back again. That got her attention, all right.

"That is not her true name," she says. Her voice is hesitant, as though she isn't sure she should be honest with me. "Did she give it to them?"

"No." I shake my head. "I don't think so."

Relief flares in her features. It's strange seeing her vulnerable. In that moment, she looks almost human. "Good."

Aleah's mother clearly knows more than she's letting on.

"What's going on?" I demand. "It was necromancer magic piloting that rogue. I saw the purple trace. Whoever it was *spoke* to me through the loup. Something, or someone, is creating these *abominations*, as you call them. That much is clear. Who is it, and why do they need her name? Why do they need her at all?"

The woman opens her mouth and closes it again. She appears to be considering how to answer. Finally, she says slowly, "You are correct. We believe there are a group of magical beings—a conclave—who wish to destroy the Accord. To do that fully, they need a banshee child's true name, together with her blood."

My mouth drops open at her words. "But why?" I push. "Why a banshee? Why not any fae, or...or *my* name, for that matter?"

I would gladly draw the danger toward me, if it would help save Aleah. *Would have helped.* Nausea threatens. *Please let it not be too late for her. Please let the fae have reached her in time.*

The woman shakes her head, her long, luscious hair moving gracefully with every turn.

"There is great power in any name, Luc Durand, but particularly that of a banshee," she says. Her voice is still guarded but there's a gentleness there I don't expect. "We are not like other fae. We carry the life and death of whole species in our hearts and in our blood. A banshee's true name in the wrong hands would unlock access to the darkness within our blood. Even a hybrid...*especially* a hybrid...the addition of human blood amplifies the very thing that they are after."

"Why Aleah in particular?" I ask.

"*All* my babies are at risk," she says through clenched teeth. Her nostrils flare. "But as to why her in particular... I believe that is on *you*, or at least, your Maker. Her father may have been chosen at random as a victim, but her cry was heard before the protector managed to blast her into silence to hide it."

"Wait." I narrow my eyes. "She has a protector? A *fae* protector?"

"Had. I dismissed him after a couple of years when nothing seemed amiss." She waves a casual hand. "And it is now on those of you remaining in this world to find who would seek the power, and ensure you destroy them, before they destroy everything you all appear to hold dear."

She disappears so quickly, even my vampiric eyesight doesn't catch the exact moment she leaves. Now I have no way to know whether the beautiful woman who saved my life not once, but twice over, will even survive the night. I don't know if I'll ever see Aleah again.

Aleah

Warmth. Pillowy softness. Light. So much light, beating back the darkness.

I open my eyes. *Am I dead? Is this heaven?*

A pale face with strong cheekbones and pointy ears appears in my vision and I jerk back and away from the stranger. *Definitely not heaven.* But I don't feel threatened.

"She's awake." The stranger speaks to someone else.

I blink and lift my head. I'm lying in a huge white bed with the softest and most comfortable mattress I've ever lain on. White netting drapes the four posts that lead up from the bed toward a ceiling somewhere far above. Presumably, anyway. There appears to be no ceiling whatsoever, only a silver mist that provides a sense of comfort despite its apparent austerity. *What the hell is this place?*

"Welcome home, Aleachiarsiwella." A woman's melodic voice washes over me, creating images in my mind of a dark-haired woman caressing my face and crooning over my cradle. Memories? A weird dream? *Mother?*

I sit up so fast a wave of dizziness hits, and I close my eyes for a second until equilibrium returns. When I open them again, I meet the curious gaze of the faerie seated in a chair beside the bed. Definitely my mother. There's no doubt in my mind that this is the woman who birthed me. It's almost like staring into a mirror. Only, this mirror is a distorted one, where the reflection staring back at me is one thousand times more beautiful than the reality.

"Hello, Mom." Gut instinct tells me she'll hate that term, and by the brief tightening of the skin around her eyes and her suddenly pursed lips, I know I've gotten it right.

A slight guffaw emerges from the dark-haired male

fae standing a few feet behind her. He must be the one who was leaning over me when I woke. My mother turns and glares at him. He returns the glare, but backs away slowly. I note his hand lifts to hide a persistent grin.

"So good to see you again after all these years." I can't seem to stop the hearty tone. There's so much emotion roiling around inside me that I don't quite know how to process it. *I died. Or so I thought. And now I'm not dead. And my mother, who I haven't seen in forever, is sitting here staring at me as if I have two heads.*

Her lips purse, but her negative reaction is brief. Annoyance makes way for apparent delight. "My darling, Aleachiarsiwella. So happy we could bring you home at last, and bring you back to the land of the living with our healing."

"It's *Aleah*, these days. Remember?" *Now let's see who can purse their lips the most out of the two of us.*

"Of course." She nods once. "But—"

"Wait. Did you say..." *Heal? Oh, my God.*

The memories come rushing back in. The crazed vamp. Luc fighting for his life. The yawning, stinky maw of that shifter...blood...darkness...the *agony* of death...

Is Luc okay? What about Laura and her son? What happened to the rogue?

I clutch at my throat, running my fingers up and down the flesh, searching for imperfection. *Nothing.* It feels completely normal. "What the actual heck?"

"Here." My mother waves her hand and an ornate, silver hand mirror materializes in the air. She leans forward to pass it to me. I double-check my neck from every possible angle, confirming what my finger exploration already revealed.

How is that possible?

"I was *dying*. I was dead." I can't even formulate the questions—how am I alive? Why am I alive? Where am I?

"No, you weren't." Her gaze flickers to her nails, perfectly manicured and painted a blood red. "I would know."

Vaguely, I recall saying something similar to Luc when I first met him, and the urge to laugh is ridiculous but strangely comforting.

"You were less than a minute away from death in the human realm, by my calculation," she continues. She drops her hand to her side and the gesture is so graceful, it's hard to acknowledge that this elegant creature is my mother. "You almost made *me* experience the banshee cry."

Mother's indignation is so strong she almost has me feeling sorry for her.

Almost. I furrow my brow and throw my legs over the side of the bed. "Hold on a—"

"Of *course*, I brought you back here." She interrupts as if I haven't spoken at all. She's still not looking at me, and I'm not sure if I should take that as regret for her actions or not. "Our magics are strongest at home, and we needed everything we had to bring you back from the brink. We almost didn't succeed."

Now she does look at me, her green eyes reflecting curiosity. I falter in my attempt to stand and instead, remain seated. I'm intimately familiar with death and well aware how close I came to losing my life. My connection to living was as tenuous as spider silk, and not nearly as strong.

I don't know how she saved me. I should be more appreciative, but in all honesty, I'm confused.

"*We?*" I narrow my eyes. "Was it you who saved my life?"

"Well." If I didn't know better, even after spending only a few minutes with this woman, I'd say my mother was embarrassed. "Tarrien did, I suppose." She casts her gaze downward at her nails once again.

Tarrien? I look beyond her to the dark-haired male fae standing several meters away. He raises a hand and tips his forehead. I nod back, and tap my heart. He lifts his brows as if surprised, and then flashes me a quick grin. *Bet dear old mom has never thanked him for anything.*

I almost feel bad for him. If he isn't appreciated by her, why does he serve her? Does he have a choice?

I'm not familiar with the ways of the fae. I'm not sure I want to be. The only thing I know of my mother was that she left my father and me to fend for ourselves.

Dear old mom is still speaking when I tune back in.

"—at my say-so, of course. He's a winter warrior, so he carries the power of healing as well as death."

I nod, crossing my arms over my chest. It's only then I realize instead of my own clothes, I'm encased in a soft white gown. I assume my mother is responsible for the change in attire, rather than the luckless Tarrien.

"Whereas your power—and mine, I guess—is only about death," I finish for her.

Her grimace seems to imply I've said something wrong and she half rises out of her seat. I've clearly hit a nerve.

"No!" She moves her arms wildly as she speaks, and yet she still appears graceful rather than aggressive or disjointed. "My power is about life, Aleachiarsiwella. As is yours. We might be destined to forever experience the banshee cry of death, but that cry is as much about life as it is about anything else. It provides the balance and harmony. Where there is life, there is also death. The yin to the yang, as the humans say. Our call provides the living with enough warning that they have a chance to say goodbye. Many don't ever have that opportunity, especially when a banshee is not there to furnish a warning."

But that's not enough. I don't want to give people the chance *to say goodbye. I want the power to* save *life. To protect the people I love.*

"Is Luc alive?" I drop my hands so they're resting on my thighs. The loose material of the gown is silky against my hands and my body relaxes a little because of it.

Mother raises a brow. How is it possible for her to convey supreme distaste in that gesture and still look elegant? It must be a practised talent mastered over the longevity of her life.

"You mean that...*vampire*?" Her mouth lifts in a sneer. "The one who was there when your father passed? Yes, he survived. Though why you'd care about a non-fae—and that particular creature especially—is beyond my understanding."

I shake my head. I misheard her, surely. She can't possibly have said that Luc was there when my father died. Luc would have told me, if that were the case. Wouldn't he?

There were two vamps, that night, a woman, and a man...

Horror punches me in the gut and I nearly lose the contents of my stomach all over this pillowy white comforter. "*Luc*...killed Dad?"

Chapter Ten

Luc—the man I allowed to take my virginity? The one I thought I could love. *He's alive.* Relief fills me, followed by horror. *He killed Dad. But he made it. He made it. He's alive.* A roller coaster of emotions washes over me. *It's not possible. Is it? Surely, he didn't...he's alive. He made it.*

I don't realize I'm holding my stomach, rocking back and forth and moaning, until she gently takes my hands and forces me to stillness.

"Stop, child. You're embarrassing yourself, and me, in front of others." She glances over at the winter warrior. "Your supernatural lover is still alive. And no, he didn't kill your father. Why do you have to be so dramatic?"

"Are you serious?" I stare at her, finally seeing her true nature. Seeing beyond the surface beauty that presumably attracted my father, to the cold and calculating creature that lies beneath. It is as if the deceptive silver mist has cleared. This banshee—this woman who birthed me—is not a nice creature at heart. She doesn't care about anything except herself, and clearly, she receives enjoyment from baiting me.

I refuse to let her have that hold on me.

For the first time in my life I'm happy she left when she did. Imagine being raised here, in this cold, empty place by a woman clearly without empathy for others? I'm glad I was raised by my human half of the family. Even if my aunt was less affectionate toward me than she would have been if I were one hundred per cent human, she never deliberately said or did anything to make me feel bad. She never manipulated me and my feelings.

"If he didn't kill Dad, then who did? And how do *you* know about it? Why was Luc there?"

The answer to that final question is more important than why or how I ended up in the faerie realm.

She shrugs. "His Maker went rogue and partnered with a were shifter," she says casually, as though the whole episode is of no consequence. "Together, they killed many innocent humans before your pet vampire brought them down."

He brought down his own Maker? Veronique, the woman he professed to love. I can't even imagine the horror he must have felt at having to take such action. *Oh, Luc.*

I wish he had told me the truth.

Would it have mattered? Would anything he said have actually changed things?

I want to see him. I want to hold him. I want to confirm for myself that he really is alive. I rub my palms on my thighs to keep them from doing something else. Like delivering a slap to my mom's cheek.

Thoughts tumble through my brain. I don't really understand. Another rogue pairing? This sounds too strange to be a coincidence. Has this current strangeness in the world been going on for twenty-five years? Is it more common than everyone believes? Why wouldn't he tell me *that*, if not the rest?

I think back to how quickly he disappeared out the door after he discovered my dad had been killed by a female vamp. There was opportunity then to mention it, surely? What stopped him? What made him run? Was it guilt? Was he afraid? Of what?

My eyes narrow at my mother. "And how do *you* know this?" I ask. I stop rubbing my hands on my dress. I push up so I'm standing. I don't come to her height and I definitely don't have her grace, but I hold my own, and I won't back down from her even if she is intimidating.

Mother stands and begins to pace the bedroom, if that's what this strange mist-filled room can be called. I step back, and let myself take in this room that I've woken up in. There's a bed, and a chair and side table, but beyond that, nothing but white-tiled floor and a ring of archways around the perimeter, each guarded by a faerie in armor. Is that for protection, or to keep me imprisoned?

"I was not there, but others were," she says. "I had someone watching over you back then, to ensure your continued safety. I arrange protection for all my babies. Your true names are powerful and in the wrong hands, can be used for ill."

It's strange to hear her say she's concerned for us. Or at least, our names. I don't even know who *us* is. From the sound of it, I have brothers or sisters scattered across the country.

I think on what she says about our names.

Your true names are powerful and in the wrong hands, can be used for ill.

What in fucking hell does that mean? I try to process her words as well as this overall situation, but it's all becoming a little too much. I don't really understand anything at the moment, and quite frankly, I just want to return home and check on Luc.

"It's a lot."

"I beg your pardon?" She furrows her brow and turns to me, annoyance marring her perfect features. "Speak up, child. Your voice may not work fully in the human realm but it should work perfectly well here at home."

"Nothing." The word is petulant as it falls out of my mouth, but I don't care. Part of me wants to smack this goddamn woman. Instead, I take a deep breath, and then another. *Okay. Calm.* Even though I don't like her, she's helping me. She saved me. And she's answering questions. "Do you confirm that Luc didn't kill dad, but instead, he killed the person who did?"

At her nod, I add, "He killed his own *Maker*?"

I still can't comprehend the difficulty of that decision. I wish we'd had the chance to talk about it before everything kicked off and turned to chaos.

"Yes." She shrugs and moves on to another subject, as if Luc and his potential angst is of no consequence. As if my father's death and the creatures who caused it are entirely unimportant. I guess, to her, these things don't matter. "It's good to see you healed, Aleah. Isn't it lucky we found you in time to bring you back to the Court?"

Good to see me? If that's true, why not make more of an effort before now?

"Ah. Yes. Lucky." I look down at my hands and shift my weight. No matter what I might feel about her, the fact that I'm alive right now is clearly testament to her intervention. And the fae who saved me, of course. "Thank you for saving my life, *Mom*."

"Stop," she snaps, her lips curling over her teeth like she's some kind of predator bearing her fangs. "It's Renna. Call me Renna."

I nearly roll my eyes. Nice to finally know my mother's name at the age of twenty-nine. I'm guessing it's not her *true* name, though, if she's so hung up about that topic.

"Which Court, um...Renna?"

"Winter, of course." She says it as though it's obvious, as though she's embarrassed that I don't know this. "You're a *banshee*."

I blink. I never thought I'd agree with her, but I should have known that. Winter makes perfect sense. Death is the ultimate ending, and yet there are many who also believe it is only the beginning.

"I guess being a banshee could fit equally well in the Spring Court," I say, more to myself than to her.

"Don't be ridiculous," my mother responds. "There're only two courts in our realm—Winter, or Summer. No in-between. Fall sits with us, and Spring with the other."

Well, *okay*. You learn something new every day.

"So, this is Winter, and you live here, now?" I face her, not sure if I want to check out a part of my heritage I never considered before this moment, or if I just want to head straight home to my own world. *And Luc.* The decision is a no-brainer, really. But the curiosity lingers.

"I've always lived here. I visit the human world only to create more of *us*. It's the task I've been given by the King, himself." Pride laces her tone. "Banshees are fading out, Aleah, and it is my duty to re-populate however I can. You have several half-brothers and sisters in the human realm. Likely another in around eight months' time."

She lays a hand on her abdomen and I have to fight hard not to cringe. She's expecting? *Ew!* Which poor human sucker has impregnated her this time? How long will she hang around in the child's life before she says sayonara and disappears yet again, leaving a baby without a mother and without the knowledge of what he or she really is?

Is it easy to leave us?

I swallow back the bitter words and aim for general nicety instead. "Congratulations."

She smiles widely and strokes her belly. "Thank you," she says. "At first, I thought one or two of you would do, but once I started it seemed like a good idea to keep going. Plus, humans make very good lovers."

She gives me a wicked grin, and I look away, trying not to cringe.

Too much information.

"Right. Okay. So, how do I get out of here?" I sweep out my arms to gesture around the room. "Where's the door? I think it's time for me to head home."

I really need to see Luc, and talk to him about what happened twenty-five years ago in my dad's apartment. In *my* apartment. I need to hear it from him. I need to know what happened.

I head determinedly across the tiled floor, searching vainly for a door. Which of the many archways leads to the exit? Or maybe there is no exit. Do they all simply teleport in and out of this place?

A wide-shouldered fae steps forward as I reach one of the archways, blocking my departure. He looks to my mother and awaits her response.

Dear old Mom glides up and gives an affirmative nod, and he steps back.

"Which way?" I don't mean to sound terse, but this place is not conducive to calm and relaxing. At least, it isn't for me. Or maybe it's just being around my mother.

"Here." She touches my arm and guides me to the left. "Come, you can at least see a little of home before you run away."

Run away. I shouldn't be surprised by this. More manipulation. However, it almost sounds as though she's disappointed that I want to leave so soon.

We step into a long corridor of what appears to be a grand home or perhaps a castle. As we pass an opening in the wall—a window without glass—I glance out on a world filled with silver-white wonder. Snow-covered grounds and thin trees bare of leaves shouldn't be so beautiful, but my heart lifts at the sparkle of light twinkling among the branches. It's the effect of sunlight arrowing its weak, winter beam through icicles dripping from the trees.

The view is picture-postcard-perfect and for the first time since I woke, I feel a faint sense of connection. "This is beautiful, Renna."

I feel a sense of peace here. I am surprised by this connection and I slow down my pace so I can truly take in the beauty that makes up a home I never had the chance of knowing.

"It is." For the first time, her tone reflects true happiness. Pride. Perhaps a twinge of regret. Perhaps she wishes I had been privy to this before now, and under less dire circumstances. "And now that I brought you here, you will always be able to return if you wish. Despite your half-breed status, your fae blood is strong. All you will need to do is remember this view and this emotion, and you will find the path back to Faerie."

She rests her hand briefly over my heart.

The walls disappear and morph into a doorway, and we enter what appears to be a large throne room filled with people. These people, though, are clearly all fae. Tall, pale and ethereal in their beauty, both men and women alike glide around with movements that seem effortless and smooth. Some have dark hair like that of my mother and me, but others are as pale blonde as possible. All have the trademark pointed ears and high cheekbones that denote a full-blood fae.

While they acknowledge Renna with polite smiles and small nods, they appear to ignore me completely. It's probably because I'm not like them, not completely.

I finger my own ears, glad in one sense that I inherited my father's normal, human-shaped ears, but

I feel so out of place here that I surreptitiously rearrange my hair to cover the anomaly. Everyone seems busy, intent on whatever business takes them scurrying through the space, but there are clusters of fae chatting and laughing and at the end of the great hall, a dais where two enormous thrones sit empty.

Another pang of longing hits me. I try to ignore it, but I can't. Despite the fact that I appreciate where I grew up, how I grew up, I can't help but feel as though I missed out on learning an important part of who I am.

I nod at the thrones. "Are they for the Winter King and Queen?"

I've not heard anything about Faerie other than what I've read or seen on television, and most of those speculations are based on human imagination, rather than reality.

Renna laughs, the sound joyous and carefree. "Oh, Aleah." She regards me with sparkles in her eyes, and I'm suddenly aware how easily she must have seduced my father and the other men she procreated with. "I didn't realize how little you know."

Well, whose fault is that, woman? I don't say my thoughts out loud, but I do raise a pointed brow when I turn to stare at her, and after a moment her cheeks turn a delicate pink. At least she has the decency to look away.

"Yes, well..." She clears her throat. "The Winter Court no longer has a Queen. King Tryppton banished her years ago, when he discovered her in bed with her warrior protector. The king is currently in the market for a new consort. There's a ball next week to introduce the current round of suitors." Her gaze turns calculating. "Hmm. Maybe..."

"Absolutely not." Somehow, I know exactly where she's going with this, and I won't have it. I will not let her use me like some kind of pawn in her little power games. "Besides, I'm sure Faerie wouldn't want a half-breed on the throne. No one likes a half-breed, do they?"

Except, perhaps, a certain vampire police sergeant. The thought of Luc sends a pang right to my heart. Where is he right now and what is he doing? Does he wonder where I disappeared to? Does he even know I'm still alive? Has he managed to survive since I was brought here?

"How long have I been here, Mo—I mean, Renna?"

"You were unconscious for four days," she says. She talks about my incapacitation like she might talk about the weather. "Your wound was severe, Aleah, as was your loss of blood. It took all of our healing magics to repair the damage to your throat. Not a bad job, if I do say so myself."

Four days. That's not so bad. Unless... "Is time the same here as it is there?"

"You mean, in the human realm?" She arches a brow as we continue to walk down the long hallway.

I'm still struck by the peaceful scenery outside. It

pulls my attention from my mother and what she's saying.

"Sometimes, but not always. Time is less...rigid here. Four days, four weeks..." She waves a hand. "Could be four years, I suppose. When you return, you'll know."

Four years? I blink. I rip my eyes away from the snow-filled landscape and turn to look at her. He could be with someone else. He could be *dead*. There's no way he would wait around for me. We were together for one night. One night and that's it.

"I appreciate you bringing me here and healing my wound, but please, I need to get home as soon as possible."

My mother pouts daintily. "You're no fun. Your father was the same. Very staid and proper." She sighs heavily, and just as I'm about to insist, she adds, "All right. Just think of the location you wish to be. Think of exactly where you want to be, and with my magic to boost you..." She lays a hand on my forearm. "There. Now think of a location and the magics will guide you along the faerie paths."

Guess I wasn't far wrong with my teleporting joke.

I hesitate. I stare at my mother, at the woman I never thought I'd actually meet. Part of me wants to immerse myself in this land, to understand a part of me I never dreamed I would have the chance to know. And now that I have it, now that I'm here, it's more difficult to say goodbye than I thought it would be.

But seeing Luc means more to me than anything else.

I close my eyes and fill my mind with thoughts of Luc. I don't know where he is now, or even when *now* actually is for him, but I hope and pray he has remained in Hatton Grove.

Silver light bursts behind my eyes, growing and spreading until there is nothing *but* the light. I open my eyes and the light recedes until I'm standing in the dark. It is the dark of night. I'm back in my own world, in my front garden at Hatton Grove. *Home.*

Luc is seated on the front porch stairs, his head in his hands. As I take a step forward his head whips up, nostrils flaring, and he stares at me with obvious shock.

"Aleah? You're...*alive*?"

A blur and he's on me, lifting me into a tight hug and squeezing so hard I can no longer breathe.

LUC

She's not dead. She's not dead. I seriously can't believe it.

I'm so happy to see her alive I begin squeezing the life out of her.

"Stop—Luc—can't...breathe."

Hell! I release the pressure of my embrace. It's just hard for me to believe that she's here, that she's real. I'm almost afraid that she'll turn into mist and leave me once again.

"Sorry, I—I thought you were dead." I take a step back so I can really look at her. She's even more perfect than I remember. "I thought you died, and she took you back to...well, to wherever fae go when they die."

When Aleah's mother first took her away, I hoped against hope that she had taken her to Faerie for healing. When she didn't return, hope began to fade. I don't know why I chose to stay here in the middle of nowhere. I think her cats appreciated the company, even if they still don't like me much. I made sure to feed them.

"They used fae magics to heal me," she says, though I can tell by the tilt of her head that she still seems confused by what happened. "I couldn't believe it either, when I woke up. I'm fine, Luc. I'm alive, and I'm truly fine, I promise."

Eventually I let her down, but keep her in the circle of my arms. It feels good to hold her solid warmth against me. I close my eyes. I try to memorize the feeling. I never want to let her go again.

"Wow, you've lost weight, Luc." Her hands flutter over my ribs, and exploratory fingers knead my back. "Haven't you been...feeding?"

I shrug. "I waited here seven weeks, just in case you returned. I fed your cats. They almost tolerate me, now. But feeding myself didn't seem as important as waiting to find out if you had...survived." The despair grew every night she didn't return. "But when time passed and you didn't reappear..."

"I can't believe that woman didn't send word to let you know I made it," she says, her fists balled at her sides. She releases a hefty sigh. "On second thought, knowing a little more about my mother, I *can* believe it now. Wait, seven weeks? What's the date?"

When I tell her, her mouth drops open. "The attack happened *two months* ago?" She runs her fingers through her hair and steps back. "It's been only a few days for me, Luc. I woke from a four-day coma—well, a healing sleep they called it—this morning. Wow. Time really does work differently in the fae realm."

I don't care how long or short it has been. She's here, and breathing, and now I have the chance finally to ask for forgiveness.

"We need to talk, Allie." Even I'm surprised by how serious I sound. I don't want to worry her but I need her to understand.

"Hmm." She disentangles from my embrace and steps back, crossing her arms in front of her. "That we do."

There's awareness in her eyes.

"You know?" I swallow but it does nothing for my dry throat.

"Renna took great pleasure in telling me you were there at my father's death," she says, her words short but not angry.

"No! At least, that's not quite how it was. I—"

"I know what happened." She steps closer until her hands rest on my chest. "I'm so sorry, Luc. Sorry that you had to be the one to...um...."

My flinch is instinctive. Even after all these years, the guilt is like a gut-wrench of pain. She's trying to spare my feelings, but maybe it's finally time to face them squarely.

"The one to kill my Mistress?" I ask. The words are easier to admit than I expect. "Yes. It was the most difficult decision I've ever had to make. No choice though, in the end. Veronique went rogue."

"She and another?" Aleah asks. Her gaze is full of sympathy and compassion. "Working in tandem, like the ones in this area?"

"Yes, exactly like that. And it wasn't as if Veronique showed any signs of madness in advance. One night she was her usual self, holding court at the house and barking orders like she did every evening in our Melbourne nest. The next night when we all woke, she was gone and the killing spree began."

Memories of family—the only family I've known since my turning—cause a pang in the region of my heart.

"I had no idea, until you mentioned it after our lovemaking, that you were the banshee baby everyone talked about after your father's death."

She shivers, and moves away from me to take a seat on the top porch step. "What did everyone say?"

"They said the banshee child cried out when Veronique entered the apartment," I say quietly. "She cried out to sing of death and sound a warning to her father, but a blast of protective power silenced the child."

"Protective power?" She wrinkles her forehead. "Someone took out my *voice*?"

"Your mother," I say. "Or at least, someone she appointed to watch over you."

Aleah's shoulders droop. It seems as though this

information has completely gutted her. "I don't whether to love or hate that woman."

She drops her face into her hands.

"For what it's worth, they do say that, without the protection, the baby would surely have died as violently as the father," I tell her. "They didn't know you were there at first and I believe that is what saved you." My voice is tentative. It's hard for me to say this at all, especially knowing Aleah was that baby and she could have died a violent death because of my Mistress. "The baby—or rather, *you*—would have been drained and left a husk. So, I guess that protection did save your life that day."

"Or—" Her voice is low, spilling out between the fingers still covering her face. "Perhaps the baby was saved because a decent vampire swept in and took action. Action that went against every grain of his being. Action that involved a life and death decision between saving a human life, and destroying the Mistress he loved—the woman who gave *him* life. Perhaps that's why I'm alive and sitting here with you today."

She lifts her head up and locks eyes with me. Those beautiful eyes are unflinching, unblinking. I can't help but return her gaze, even though it pierces me to my core.

"Perhaps."

"Oh, Luc." She lowers her hands from my chest. She's so close now, we're nearly kissing. How badly I want her to kiss me. How badly I want to lose myself in her. "I may have saved your life in recent times, but I suspect, twenty-five years ago, your actions saved mine. And most likely, many other innocent lives as well."

The thought that it was my action that contributed to letting Aleah live all those years ago eases the ache that invaded my soul when I thought she was dead. I take a seat beside her on the step. Where our thighs touch, heat ignites.

"I think I still owe you one," I tell her. "Or at least, I definitely owe your bees."

She smiles at me, and the vision is priceless. "I thought that was a hallucination. My dying brain playing tricks on me."

"Nope." I shake my head, glad to see her smile. "Without the intervention of your bees I would not be here now. How did you do that?"

"I have no idea. I just called them in my mind. Asked them to protect the one I—" Her cheeks transform from pale to an attractive shade of pink. Instead of looking at me, she looks down at her hand. She picks at her dress—a beautiful white silky thing that reminds me of distant human memories of clouds in the sky on a particularly bright day.

I knock her gently with my shoulder. "The one you...*like?*" I tease. "Maybe just a little?"

She stares down at her feet. "The one I like more than a little." Her voice is strained but rough. Honest. "The one I like quite a goddamn lot."

I place a finger under her chin, forcing her face back up to meet my gaze. I hope she can read my conviction when I nod and say, "I like you a lot, too, Aleah. More than a lot. When I thought you were dead —" A shudder shakes my frame, and she rests a gentle hand on my thigh and leans her head on my shoulder. The pain of loss dissipates.

"I'm not planning to go anywhere, Luc." Her voice is firm. "How about you?"

"I can't promise to be here every night. It is the nature of my work to have to travel. We still haven't gotten to the bottom of whatever or whoever is controlling the rogues. Or turning supernaturals into rogues in the first place."

She nods. "I think it might be necromancer magic."

"How do you know that?" I lean back so I can watch her reaction. I can't exactly read her face, but I'm curious to know how she came to this conclusion.

"I saw it, that night." Her gaze is suddenly far away, as though she's remembering. "I thought it was part of my dying. The purple haze...it seemed to be winning, devouring you. I'm so glad it didn't."

"Hmm. Me too." *Necromancer magic.* The fact that Aleah saw it too makes me certain my guess is correct. "We found a medallion at the site of your neighbors' murder—a pendant with an unusual and intricate pattern. We think either Darrie or Gwen tore it off one of their attackers in the frenzy."

She nods slowly. "Laura said something about that.

With everything else that happened, I never got the chance to ask you about it."

"It's back at SUDAP now, in the secure facility in Melbourne. They're still working on unlocking the pendant's secrets."

She shifts as if restless. "Did you touch it?"

"No."

"Good. Not sure why that matters, but I feel like it does."

"It felt wrong when I first saw it lying there in the dirt. Wrong...like...bad magic." A shiver traverses my skin. *Very bad magic.*

"The thing is," I add, shifting a lock of hair behind her ear. "I saw another medallion, on the vamp that tried to kill you."

Her eyebrows rise up toward her hairline. I don't want to scare her, but after all Aleah has been through, it seems petty to keep anything back at this point.

"I believe there's a hidden agenda that is playing out here. An agenda that relates to the Accord. Someone, or a group of people, are trying to work against everything the Accord stands for. Possibly led by a necromancer who is creating the loups and controlling them somehow via the pendants. Your mother mentioned a movement against the Accord—a Restoration, she called it."

"*Mother* knows what's going on?"

"Only snippets, I believe. My team will need to investigate further. But at least now we're no longer proceeding completely blind." I cover her hand where it rests on my thigh and interlace our fingers. "While I will still need to travel, I do need a base...a place that... perhaps I might call...*home*?"

She raises our interlinked hands to her lips and drops a kiss on the top of my knuckles, one by one. The gesture sends tentacles of warmth reaching into every part of my cold vampire body. The residual unease that rose when I mentioned the medallion seems to dissipate into thin air. It feels so good to be warm. It feels so good to be with Aleah. It feels so good to finally, once again, feel *alive*.

"You *are* home, Luc. If you want. You have my permission to enter or leave this place as you wish. I rescind my own power to rescind the invitation. There. What do you say about—"

I end her inane chatter with a kiss that feels like everything I've ever wanted wrapped up in this one connection. Her mouth, her lips, her generous heart— even the strange gift of her banshee cry. I accept everything she has to offer, and give all that I have in return. *Home.* Yes, I truly believe I may have finally found my place.

And in this moment, I realize I'm hopeful for the first time in a long, long while.

Epilogue

TARRIEN

Neither of the creatures sharing a passionate kiss appear to have sensed my presence. Lady Renna bade me be discreet and no one, not even an armored winter warrior like myself, wants to end up on the wrong side of an enraged banshee's temper. Especially Lady Renna's.

My brief is to watch for danger, protect if needed, and above all else, don't let the hybrid know of my presence.

The vampire is more problematic. If Aleah were full-blood fae, she would sense my proximity in a heartbeat. Vampires, as a species, are generally far less skilled than fae in terms of their ability to detect the ancient magics, but this one in particular has a keener sense than most. I worry he may detect me at some point.

I roll my eyes as their kiss progresses to fondling. This is not a warrior's task, to stand and watch others making love. And yet here I am, stuck until my brief changes and I am handed a new—and hopefully more suitable—task.

I touch the moonstone that sits in the silver filigree ring on my right thumb. The gem is a vehicle for communication, and it doesn't take long before the air shimmers and Renna appears by my side.

"What is it, Tarrien? Can you not manage without me for more than a few minutes?"

My lip curls up in annoyance. *Oh, how I dislike this woman.*

"Depends on your point of view." I wave my hand, indicating the couple on the porch stairs now in the throes of tearing off each other's clothing, and Renna takes a tiny step back.

"Oh!" she says. Then her face clears and interest overtakes the shock. "Well. She seems to be doing all right for herself, doesn't she? Truly, the vampire is not bad-looking at all. Hmm...his rear end is particularly shapely, now that he is free of his clothing."

She leans forward. *Not okay, woman. She's your daughter.* I drag at her arm, eventually managing to turn her attention back to me.

"Do you seriously expect me to stay here and watch over *this*, Renna?" I try to keep the attitude from my voice, but it's difficult.

She is quiet for a moment, closing her eyes and sniffing the air. "Can't sense anything odd in these parts, any longer. Maybe they *will* be fine, after all. *Maybe...*" She taps her lips thoughtfully, and then nods in a decisive manner. "Yes. I've decided. I want to relieve you of your duty here, Tarrien."

Well, thank the winter gods for that. About time. I turn, readying to leave for home, when she stops me in my tracks with her next words. "Instead, I need you to visit Melbourne and check on Indigo's welfare. I've been getting bad vibes about some of my other children. Should have had you check on Indie a while back, but to be honest—" She laughs lightly. "After my visit when she was seven, I forgot she existed."

I should be surprised by this admission, but I'm not. "How old is she now?"

Renna counts mentally. "Hmm. Must be thirty? Perhaps thirty-one. She came prior to Aleah."

Distaste once again curves my mouth. This woman is seriously hideous, but thanks to my father's infatuation with the winter queen and his subsequent betrayal of our family and the whole Winter Court, my family now owes Lady Renna a blood debt. She unexpectedly spoke up for us when no one else would, and it is now incumbent upon me, the first-born, to fulfil that debt. If I do not, innocent members of my family will be killed, and we will lose our place at Court. That last fact alone would probably kill my mother.

"If I do this for you, my family debt will be paid, Renna. I have given you years in return for your action on our behalf. *Years.*"

"Of course. Now off with you, Tarrien, and report back via the usual channels." She points at my moonstone and touches the matching gem at her neck, and then is gone before I can answer.

Fucking banshee witch.

I cast one last look at the couple making love on the porch. They seem well-matched and Aleah's silver-white aura has extended to encompass the vamp. A sure sign that she has begun to find true happiness with her mate.

I'm glad for her. There was a moment there, in Faerie, when her kindness touched me more than I expected. She seems nothing like her mother, thankfully. Instead, she seems like the kind of creature I wouldn't mind getting to know.

I wonder if I will ever find someone who provides such happiness for me? As a winter warrior, my heart is, of necessity, cased in ice. We are protectors, not lovers, and it is our duty to ignore the call of the flesh as much as it is within our power to do so.

My father's weakness in giving in to his passions—despite being a winter warrior himself—is what destroyed our family's reputation in the first place.

Indigo. Indie. The name sends skitters of energy across my skin. Interesting. Will the hybrid prove to be more like her mother, or her half-sister? Or will she be nothing like either?

I turn my thoughts toward Melbourne and a human-fae hybrid named Indigo.

The End

Sneak Peek of Banshee Song

I hope you enjoyed this first instalment in THE BLOOD FAE CHRONICLES. Read Indie and Tarrien's story in BANSHEE SONG, and then Maewen and Rhodri's story in BANSHEE POWER. These stories are best read in order.

Here's a small taste of BANSHEE SONG...

Indigo

The last note dies away and silence fills the theater. The quality of that silence is sharp and expectant, as if everyone in the audience is holding their breath and waiting for more.

There is no more. Not for these humans. If I truly

gave them everything I have, there'd be no silence. Only terrified screams, and the rush of bodies toward the exit. Away from the horror. Away from me.

Slowly the applause begins, escalating as the audience rises to their feet. A standing ovation. I must have excelled, tonight. I lift my chin and gaze out past the stage lights to acknowledge the accolades directed my way.

"Bravo, brava, huzzah..."

The shouts vary from person to person, but all convey essentially the same message. I delivered what this audience wanted, and then some.

"Encore, encore..."

I incline my head, blinking hard to force back the threatening tears. Do they know I sing of death? Do they know I sing of loss and all things that might be and never eventuate? Do they know how much it costs me, every time I stand up here on this stage, to croon the song of every human passing?

The power of a banshee is beyond any mortal understanding.

The power of a banshee's voice is beyond the understanding of all of them, mortal and immortal alike.

Of course, I'm only a half-banshee. But even so, I have to rein in my voice to deliver as much as they can take, and not a single note more.

The threat of tears eases and this time when I raise my head, confidence fills me. It will be okay. Tonight, will be okay. There is no one nearby who needs the call of the banshee this evening.

As I take one more bow and turn to leave the stage, a spark of silver from someone in the front row catches and holds my attention. A set of steel-gray eyes meet mine, and for the briefest moment my heart does a strange flip-flop in my chest. A tall man—taller than those around him by at least a head—continues to slow clap in what seems like a parody of the adulation around him.

His hair is dark and long, pulled back in an elegant ponytail. Like everyone else I can see in the limited reach of the stage lights, he's sporting evening wear, but this man gives off the impression that he is only here under sufferance.

A sparkle emanates from a ring on one of his fingers. Another flash from the piece of jewelry holds my gaze. Who is he? And why is he looking at me that way, as if he knows me and doesn't like what he sees?

The sardonic twist of his lips sends a different message altogether to the continued and almost offensive slow clap.

I'm certain, even in the glance I give him before leaving the stage, that he's not human.

Elf? Fae? The slightly pointed ears, aristocratic nose, and high cheekbones could be either, but elves are usually light-haired, not dark, and fae can be either. Which means this guy is likely pure fae.

Awesome. If there's anything I hate more than a

cynical man, it's a cynical man with fae blood running through his veins.

About the Author

Jen Katemi is a *USA Today* bestselling author of steamy contemporary and paranormal romance. She is published with Evernight Publishing, and previously as Jennifer Lynne with Red Sage. Jen also has forged a successful indie career starting with her popular BLOOD FAE CHRONICLES, GODS OF LOVE and FORBIDDEN series.

When she's not writing, Jen looks after the family, pampers various cats, and tries to find a smidgen of time for her husband. She lives in Melbourne, Australia.

Visit Jen's website to sign up for her reader newsletter and never miss a new release.

www.JenKatemi.com